Crackodile

GARY LEE VINCENT

Burning Bulb
PUBLISHING

Crackodile
By **Gary Lee Vincent**

Burning Bulb Publishing
P.O. Box 4721
Bridgeport, WV 26330-4721
United States of America
www.BurningBulbPublishing.com

First Edition.

Paperback Edition ISBN: 978-1-948278-63-8

Also by Gary Lee Vincent

Novels
PASSAGEWAY
BELLY TIMBER
ATTACK OF THE MELONHEADS
WHEN THE BEDPOSTS SHAKE (RING OF THE SUCCUBUS)
IMPOUND
STRANGE FRIENDS
THE BEST ACTORS THAT EVER LIVED
THE BLIND MELODY
JEROME

Darkened—The West Virginia Vampire Series
DARKENED HILLS
DARKENED HOLLOWS
DARKENED WATERS
DARKENED SOULS
DARKENED MINDS
DARKENED DESTINIES

The Douglas River Vampire Series
RIVER: A VAMPIRE'S NIGHTMARE
ICARUS

The Crackimals Series
CRACKCOON
CRACKODILE

Dedicated to
Daniel Brooks

CHAPTER 1

The time was about a quarter to six on a warm summer Saturday evening. The place was the Exotic Wonders Animal Clinic on the outskirts of Zanesville, Ohio.

Walt Pollak backed his long black van up to the rear entrance of the animal clinic.

"Hey, easy," his brother Jake cautioned him, when the rear of the vehicle almost clipped a railing on the service ramp adjacent to the passenger side.

The clinic building sat on several acres of land near Interstate 70. The clinic was surrounded by animal cages of various shapes, with the habitat environment each cage contained being fitted to a variety of animal and bird species. The arrangement of cages formed a horseshoe shape around the central building.

At the moment most of the cages stood empty, though a few recovering 'patients' like a pair of macaws and two monkeys stared at the arriving vehicle from the branches of encaged trees on opposite sides of the driveway.

"And . . . we're good," Jake said as the van came to a final stop two yards from the door. Next, Jake looked over at his brother. "Is Tom gonna be waiting for us here?"

Walt shook his head. "Nah, bro. He's at the wedding reception with all the others."

Jake smiled and rubbed his hands together. "Wow, this is a sweet deal then. A real piece of cake. And I ain't talkin' 'bout wedding cake."

Walt nodded. "Yeah, it is. So long as we don't fuck it up."

The two brothers pulled on black ski-masks and gloves and then pushed open their respective van doors and got out. Then they each

1

walked along the van to meet up at the clinic's rear entrance. For a while, both men stood concealed from view by the long bulk of the van, cautiously appraising the lay of the land, watching both the surrounding forests and cages, in case any observers were nearby.

"I think we're alone here," Walt said finally. "How 'bout you? You see anything suspicious?"

Jake shook his head. "Nah. Coast is clear. Everyone's gotta be over at the wedding in Columbus."

"Well, here goes," Walt said, stepping away from the van towards the clinic's rear double doors, which were like those of a human ER, but wider, since they had to admit elephants if necessary. "I just hope Tom didn't forget to leave the rear door unlocked again."

"Like the time with the ocelot?" Jake shook his head. "Nah, I doubt that'd be the case. He's still bummed out that we lost that deal; and this time too much cash is at stake for Tom to screw up—remember he's always bitching about his child support payments."

Walt nodded. "Even so . . . ." Then he shrugged. "Let's do this, bro." After a last cautionary glance at the nearby cages and the forest beyond, he hurried over to the rear entrance and tested the lock. The doors opened easily.

"We're good to go," he informed his brother. "Let's get that damn gurney out of the van."

***

The Pollak brothers were criminals. Older brother Walt was short, dark, and stocky, and in his pre-crime existence had been a forest ranger. However, after a decade of lazy and undistinguished service to West Virginia's forest and wildlife, Walt Pollak had discovered a cheaper way to make money: by selling stolen wildlife to private zoos. There was always someone somewhere who was willing and desperate enough to pay an arm and a leg for some exotic animal or bird species, and Walt had discovered that since, unlike humans, animals couldn't exactly be fingerprinted, all he had to do to stall the investigation was move the animal in question across state lines. All lions looked alike; so did all zebras, and monkeys, etc. Walt stole the desired animal and delivered it, and collected the money, which he then shared with his younger brother Jake.

Jake Pollak looked a lot like Walt, but was about a foot taller. Where Walt was the brains of the animal-thieving team, Jake was the muscle. Jake also wasn't very smart and since their teens, had shown no desire to do any honest work. So stealing and reselling animals fit him very well.

The pair had been in business for a year now, and had made a good profit. They'd had a few close scrapes with the law, but so far, their good luck had held. And as Walt had already pointed out to Jake, if this evening's steal went just as smoothly, they'd each have enough cash in the bank to retire on.

***

The brothers unloaded the heavy-duty gurney from their van and rolled it through the rear doors of the clinic. A tranquilizer gun lay on top of the stretcher.

"Left or right," Jake asked as they immediately reached a T-shaped corridor.

"Right is where the interior pool is located," Walt replied.

The brothers turned right and headed fast down the clinic corridor.

"It's just occurred to me that we'd best hurry up," Walt said as they walked past an animal ward with mostly empty cages lining its walls.

"Why's that?"

"I feel weird being all alone in here with these animals. I know Tom said everyone would be at Dr. Smith's wedding, but you can be certain it's just a matter of time before one of the vets is gonna feel guilty about leaving all the animals alone for even a few hours and rush back to check on their welfare."

Jake shook his head. "No need to worry. You're forgetting what Tom told us."

"Remind me, bro."

"That except for the horses, they don't have any serious cases this week. Everything else was rescheduled to Monday because of the wedding."

Walt nodded. "Good. No one's gonna be disturbing us then."

"Not unless someone's pet lion develops indigestion."

They'd arrived at the clinic's interior pool and could now see its sole occupant.

"Damn, that thing is huge," Jake said, with a twinge of fear in his voice. "We're gonna need more tranks."

***

Bill, the Nile crocodile, was in the animal clinic by accident. The crocodile, normally a resident of the Cincinnati Zoo, had suddenly been taken inexplicably ill.

Bill, normally as violent and predatory as the rest of his species had begun refusing meals and had soon been trucked over here to have his illness diagnosed.

But an X-ray had then revealed Bill's illness to be nothing more than a kid's sneaker stuck in his gut, thankfully without its young owner attached. Even though a crocodile's digestive enzymes *are* as corrosive as generally believed, and really can digest nails (building nails, not finger ones), these modern new-fangled plastics and fabrics had proven more than a match for them. The sneaker remained undigested and thus Bill got indigestion.

Anyway, with this diagnosis reached, the ailing crocodile was then tranquilized and a modified catheter stuck down its throat and maneuvered to the obstruction. The evil little shoe was yanked out into daylight again, and the crocodile, on waking up, immediately felt better, as was evinced by his immediately trying to eat the man standing closest to him.

Bill the crocodile was still in the animal clinic because clinic boss Dr. Smith was getting married today, and all of his staff would be attending his wedding.

And so, knowing that the crocodile would be in residence at the Exotic Wonders Animal Clinic until Monday morning at least, Tom Hale, drinking buddy and criminal friend of Walt and Jake Pollak, and who also happened to be head of security at the clinic, had informed his two friends that they could have a Nile croc for the taking . . . if the buying price was right.

*****

Now, Jake pointed worriedly at the crocodile and asked his brother. "Man, are you sure this gurney's big enough?"

Walt stared appraisingly at Bill the crocodile. He understood where Jake was coming from. The photos Tom had sent them hadn't done the slightest justice to the animal they were looking at. This African crocodile was at least ten feet in length, minus its tail. And up close and personal like this, it was scary as fuck too. Walt was used to transporting smaller animals. They concealed well, and for another, were easy to put to sleep. Even the gators they'd trucked up north had been medium-sized ones.

But this thing. It's a fucking monster! It's much larger than all those gators we've moved in the past!

Seeing as he would be alone for most of the day, Bill had been thrown half of a goat and left to his own devices in the interior pool. Left alone, the croc might have been content with the goat, but on seeing the two men, he hurriedly abandoned the half consumed flesh he had been tearing into and crawled up to the stout metal poles which ringed the pool and flung his squat body against them, in a bid to attack the two intruders.

His roar as he attacked the metal poles must have been heard for miles around. At least it seemed that way to Jake, who leapt away from the poles.

"Hey, hey, boy," we ain't here to hurt you," Jake said.

"Nah, not at all," Walt agreed, staring into the crocodile's open mouth, along the twin rows of long pointy teeth in its upper and lower jaws, and down the black chasm of its throat. The sight—the thought of what those teeth could do to him—made him shudder. "Billy boy, we're just gonna move you from this derelict house to Mr. Johnson's comfy place."

Jake nodded down at the enclosed beast and added, "Yup. Mr. Johnson's offered us twenty grand if we make you a tenant of his, and we intend to collect." Then, as the crocodile gave up his attempt to break through the poles and lay down watching them hungrily, Jake frowned at Walt. "Hey, I think this creature's worth more than we're being paid for it."

Walt nodded. "Yeah, a whole lot more. Maybe a hundred grand. Tom's an idiot, he made the croc look like it was six feet long, and that's why we advertised it at that rate. He must've been drinking before or while taking the snaps."

After a quick glance at the CCTV camera out in the corridor, which Tom had ensured was angled out of their line of sight, Walt nodded to his younger brother. "Let's just get this animal loaded up and move it away from here before someone returns. We'll discuss the biz with Johnson when we're safely away. Johnson's got money to spare; he just wants the croc as a vanity piece, 'cos everyone else he knows has gators. He'll be sure to pay us something extra."

Jake nodded and picked up the tranquilizer gun.

Putting Bill the crocodile to sleep proved easy enough. Crocodiles aren't much for brains. On seeing Walt pointing the gun at him, instead attempting to hide himself away in the water, the crocodile flung himself against the bars again. Walt waited until Bill spread his jaws wide and then shot the croc in the fleshy part of its mouth. Its snout closed and then opened again, revealing the tranquilizer dart impaled like a misplaced plastic tooth in its pink mouth flesh. Just to make sure, Walt shot the crocodile in the mouth again.

Walt and Jake waited till Bill stopped thrashing and lay limp.

Once the crocodile closed his eyes, the two brothers prodded him with a wooden stick to ensure that he was really asleep. Then they retrieved the key to the pool enclosure from its hook on the wall, and unlocked its entrance.

"Let's roll him onto the gurney," Walt said, hastily rolling the gurney into the enclosure.

Jake did most of the work whilst Walt grabbed a hold of the crocodile's tail.

The job seemed to take forever, but finally they got Bill positioned on the collapsed gurney. The crocodile lay on his back, his white belly made all the whiter by the room lights. The gurney was seven feet long; Bill's head projected off of one end of it, and his tail projected off the other end. The croc was strapped down around the middle, though the bands barely managed to circle his humongous body.

With Bill's tail dragging on the floor behind them, the brothers began wheeling the unconscious animal off towards the clinic's rear entrance.

"You know," Jake said as he muscled the gurney along the deserted corridor. "I'd hate for this damn animal to suddenly wake up on us."

Walt shuddered at the thought of that happening. And right at that moment, Walt Pollak had the queer and very dreadful gut feeling that the sensible thing for he and his brother Jake to do was to return Bill the Nile crocodile back to the safety of the Exotic Wonders Animal Clinic's interior pool and get the hell away from this place.

But of course, being a crook and a very greedy one at that, Walt simply shrugged away this premonition of disaster.

He smiled down at the unconscious animal on the stretcher. *What the hell can possibly go wrong now?* he silently asked himself as they approached the rear door of the clinic and were staring into the rear of their van. *All we gotta do now is drive this croc into West Virginia and we'll be smiling all the way to the bank!*

Getting the animal loaded into the van took a while, despite the vehicle's rear ramp. The crocodile was just that big. But Jake persevered and soon, Bill, still strapped down on the gurney, was loaded up and in transit away from the Exotic Wonders Animal Clinic.

Before driving off, however, Walt shot Bill up with another dose of tranquilizer.

"Just to be on the safe side," he told Jake, as the latter forced the slumbering reptile's jaws open so they could retrieve the previous two darts from its mouth. "It's a long way over to Elkins."

"Well, bro, let's go get paid," Jake said cheerily. "Soon, we both are gonna be very rich men."

"So long as nothing goes wrong," Walt agreed. He still couldn't shake the feeling that disaster loomed along their way.

But how the hell can that be? he pondered as they joined the I-70 and began their journey to West Virginia.

CHAPTER 2

Visiting Max Carillo always left Toby Morales in a strange frame of mind, and today was no exception.

Toby and his girlfriend Denise Higgins, partners in both crime and romance, were here in Max's in descript trailer home to pick up their latest shipment of Agent Orange. The pair of them were seated in Max's living room waiting, while Max relieved himself in the bathroom.

Agent Orange was Max's brainchild, an orange-colored variant of crack cocaine that was guaranteed to make them all rich . . . once Max succeeded in ironing out the kinks in the compound's formula.

Selling Agent Orange had Toby feeling conflicted.

We're selling this shit that makes folks act crazy. It's more addictive than heroin, as bad as crystal meth even.

Now, Toby Morales was no saint. He'd done things he didn't even like thinking about, as had his girlfriend Denise. But this Agent Orange drug got him rather scared. Some folks on the street even gave it the nickname "Acid Mine Drainage" both for the phonetics of "mine" sounding like "mind" and the more disturbing side effect of orange discharge sometimes leaking from certain user's eyes and bodily orifices. Those experiencing such allergic reactions, if one could call it that, were often prone to sudden shifts of violence accompanied by mania and even death. For many in West Virginia's coal mining community, the orange sulfur runoff all too familiar in the strip mines did, in fact, resemble the orange-colored discharge.

Once you start on this, it's a total downward slide, not a spiral—that would take too long and even give you time to reconsider the downturn your life has taken; but no, Agent Orange kicks in and then kicks you like a bitch.

9

GARY LEE VINCENT

Toby didn't do any drugs other than pot; and the same went for his girl Denise. He was strict on that; he wasn't about dating an addict.

Max, however, didn't share Toby's ethical reservations.

What does Max think anyway? This was a question Toby had asked himself more than once and had asked his girlfriend too.

"He's interested in making money," Denise had replied him with admiration. "I like that about him."

"I'm interested in making money too," Toby had retorted. But I'm not about to sell my soul to the devil to get rich." Toby had been a bit drunk when they'd had this conversation, or he'd have realized that dealing drugs was exactly that; handing Satan a chunk of one's soul for safekeeping, particularly on those occasions when he 'converted' previous non-users to this way of life that was certain to ruin them.

However, Denise had quickly set him straight on that score.

"Baby," she'd said, while puffing on a joint (which Toby was fine with), "If you're not as bad as Max, why the fuck don't we just sell pot and coke then?"

Toby had hemmed and hawed, but the answer had been obvious, and so he'd not disputed it when Denise had laid it out for him.

"I'll tell you why, baby," she'd gone on. "It's because the markets for those drugs are already saturated. Agent Orange is new and gives the user an incomparable high. We're in on the ground floor and if we're smart, we can ride the elevator all the way to the top.

That much was true.

But . . . I just hate the fact that Agent Orange screws people's brains up, Toby thought, stubbornly clinging to a thread of moral superiority.

"So does just about every other illegal narcotic known to man," Max informed him then, emerging from the bathroom to a flush noise. "You name it—cocaine, crack, acid; even innocent marijuana has a reputation of destroying its users' brain cells over an extended period of time."

Toby thought he'd been keeping his thoughts to himself, but Max's comment made him realize he'd actually been thinking aloud.

10

"There's no point feeling guilty about what we're doing," Max went on. "Yeah, yeah, I know, the customer is at risk; but we're not forcing the customer to take that risk. Using Agent Orange is buying a lottery ticket. The options are simple: are you gonna have a winning experience and have one of the best drug trips of your life, or have you just wasted your damn money, and risk going nuts to boot?"

"I agreed and disagree," Denise said, running her blue eyes over Max's face. "Yeah, yeah, the user is responsible for taking those risks. But can't we make the fucking drug safer?"

"You mean, can't *I* make the fucking drug safer, don't you?" Max laughed. Max Carillo was a bearded and bespectacled man who, wearing his white lab coat, looked every inch the genius chemist that he was. His pale eyes reflected a kind of amoral intelligence that compounded Toby's concerns about the man; after Toby had hung around Max for a while, he'd reached the conclusion that Max didn't honestly care if Agent Orange was good or evil; nor did Max care if his wonder creation made him a financial killing or not. No, Max Carillo seemed more concerned with studying the effect his drug had on the people who used it.

Yeah, sure, the guy pays lip service to the idea that Agent Orange needs to be refined and made safer, but he's really enjoying his ability to play God with us 'little people.'

"C'mon, man, you must be able to do something about the side effects—particularly that uncontrollable anger," Denise said. "It's bad business for us all if our clients continually embark on killing sprees. If nothing else, it's gotten you, and by extension us as well, wanted by the police."

Max laughed. "But lady and gentleman, therein lies my genius. The cops have no idea who we are. Our clients are so scared of being cut off from their supply that they'll never rat on us. May I remind you both that I coded maximum addiction into Agent Orange." Max dipped a hand into the left pocket of his lab coat and pulled out a little chunk of orange 'candy' dusted with white powder, which he then held up to the light and turned over between his fingers. "Oh yes. Once you've had a few hits of this orange shit, you're hooked for life."

Toby felt scared on hearing this. Then the fright wore off and he felt like a hypocrite. *Because, yeah, I know I'm gonna keep pushing this orange shit on the streets, and its very capability for perfect addiction is what's gonna make me my fortune.*

"I still dislike how so many people gets angry once they use it," Denise insisted, getting up from the armchair she was seated in and peering out of a window of Max's trailer, at the boats out on Teter Creek Lake.

"Not everyone," Max corrected her a little angrily.

"But most of them do," Denise said, turning around to face him. Sitting on the windowsill, she presented her objection: "Dude, other drugs supposedly reduce or remove a user's inhibitions—like the way alcohol helps shy people to be less so in a party situation. But that stuff of yours,"—she pointed over at the little orange rocks that Max was still rolling between his fingers— "boosts violent emotions in the users." She held up a hand to prevent Max from interrupting her. "And it's not just in those people whose eyes develop an orange tint. Anyone can snap at any time."

Max laughed, showing two rows of uneven teeth. "Maybe that's part of the attractions of using Agent Orange, baby, the thrill of the uncertainty of it all."

Toby sighed. "Dude, don't you fucking care at all? The more people that kill themselves, the more the cops are gonna want us behind bars—and I'm talking the feds too now that we've begun moving stuff into Ohio, Pennsylvania, and Kentucky. Max, bro, we don't need the DEA heat."

Denise nodded. "One little slipup and we're all gonna be jailbirds."

"Yeah; then how's the stuff gonna get moved if we in jail?" Toby underscored, tapping his fingers on his knees.

"Well then, I guess it's up to you two to ensure there aren't any slipups, ain't it?"

Toby winced. The voice was unmistakable. Max's girlfriend Jessie had just stepped into the living room. Jessie Barnes was a tall and bony blonde, her anorexic look resulting from her crack addiction, which ensured she rarely ate much. She was pretty, but her looks were already fading away. She'd soon look like own mother.

Nah, Toby thought. *Soon Jessie's ma's gonna look younger than she does.*

Jessie walked over and sat on Max's lap. Her smile revealed two missing teeth and the fact that her eyes had an orange tinge to them.

Toby didn't question why Max was with Jessie. He'd heard rumors that she was fantastic in bed. He wasn't tempted to try her out however. Even if he didn't mind ruining his relationship with Max, who tended to be very possessive of Jessie, there was also Denise to consider.

Denise could charitably be described as a nympho. She wanted sex all the fucking time, and considering the sheer amount of sexual energy she drained from Toby on a regular basis, he had no energy left over to cheat on her with.

So no, Max could keep Jessie and the best of a life to them both.

"Hey, you guys, what's so bad about being angry a lot anyway?" Jessie asked. "I don't mind the feeling. Nor does Max." She leaned back and stroked his cheek with her fingernails. "Or do you, darling?"

Max quickly shook his head. "Of course not. It adds spice to our relationship."

Toby smirked. He wasn't buying that for an instant. He knew about the corpses buried beneath Max's trailer—he'd helped Max bury them. On both occasions, Jessie had snapped after using Agent Orange and stabbed someone to death. Max didn't want Jessie to go to jail and so he and Toby had buried the corpses. Both dead men had been hardcore drug users too, so there'd been no investigation into their disappearance; at least not any that had brought the police to Teter Creek Lake and Max's trailer.

True, Jessie Barnes might be the best fuck ever, but Max is delusional if he imagines she won't turn on him one day. All that Jessie needs is one trigger, and she'll turn on Max like a she-bear robbed of her cubs.

This time Toby Morales *had* successfully kept his thoughts to himself, but maybe Max felt some kind of psychic vibe leap between them both, because out of the blue, he suddenly looked pensive.

"Alright, you guys," Max said. "I don't want you both thinking I'm completely insensitive to the wellbeing of our clients. I've been working on it, trying to synthesize a variant of Agent Orange that'll lack the mental adjustment effects."

"I don't see why you need to do that," Jessie immediately said, with more than a hint of anger in her voice.

"It's just good business, darling," Max said while tapping Jessie's ass, to indicate that she get off his lap. Then he got to his feet and gestured towards the rear of his trailer. "Come on and I'll show you two what I've been up to in my lab."

Toby looked at Denise who nodded back at him. Then the pair of them got up and walked after Max and Jessie.

CHAPTER 3

Max's laboratory occupied the larger of his trailer's two bedrooms.

Walking in there one got the impression of entering a real chemical lab, what with all the tables full of scientific equipment and strangely colored liquids that foamed and bubbled in test tubes. A first-time visitor to this lab, an outsider, might have mistakenly assumed that important cancer research was being conducted in here.

It would have come as a shock to that person that all this state-of-the-art equipment had been assembled solely for the purpose of manufacturing narcotics.

But that was the state of affairs in here. All those years of Max Carillo's studying both in high school and university had resulted in this: his being about to become the premier supplier of illegal chemical substances to northeastern USA.

After which, Max had plans to export Agent Orange across the rest of the USA, and then worldwide. For that, he planned to lean on his cartel connections south of the boarder.

Toby and Denise had been in here before and had seen everything in here before, except for the row of small animal cages that were now arranged against the left wall of the converted bedroom.

Both sets of bedroom drapes were shut tight, but this was merely a formality where secrecy was concerned; the north set of drapes (the set that lay directly ahead as one entered the laboratory) concealed a view of the nearby woods (Max having sensibly bought a trailer at the fringe of the trailer camp), while the left/east set of drapes (those above the animal cages), parted to reveal Mrs. Beardsley's trailer.

Mrs. Beardsley was in her mid-sixties and was subject to partial dementia in which she constantly claimed abduction attempts by men in flying saucers. All things considered, Max couldn't have asked for a more perfect next-door neighbor.

Toby and Denise followed Max over to the cages and stopped and stared. Most of the cages contained either a rat, a rabbit, or a guinea pig. All the animals were alike in that they all had glowing orange eyes.

"Don't know why, but animals have less resistance to Agent Orange than humans do," Max said, indicating the specimens. "The anger thing is however shared."

This latter statement was quickly borne out when the little caged animals all began throwing themselves at the bars of their cages, clearly in an attempt to reach and attack the humans beyond them. As they leapt, they bared their little jaws wide and gnashed their little teeth, viciously snapping at the air.

Despite the bars preventing them leaving their confinement, the ferocity of the animal's rage was such that it caused Toby step back and Denise to cling to him in alarm.

"They're not hungry," Max pointed out unnecessarily. "They're simply enraged. I've no idea what's going on in their little heads, but it's extremely bad." He pointed over at a large pile of bloody scraps piled on a metal tray. "Behold the remains of a rabbit that hadn't been treated with Agent Orange, but which I put into a cage with one that had been treated. After killing the untreated rabbit, the treated one made no attempt to eat it, but instead did everything in its power to render it to the shredded mess that adorns that tray . . . while the other caged animals watched the show and also tried to reach them."

"That's creepy as fuck," Denise said.

"Now watch this," Jessie said. While Max had been talking, she'd been leaning on his shoulder, but now, she straightened up and stretched out a hand to her boyfriend. Max nodded and deposited a little rock of Agent Orange into Jessie's palm.

The effect of seeing the drug on the caged creatures was astounding. They each froze in their rampage against the bars of their cages and stood still as statues, while Jessie got out a crack pipe from her purse, packed it with the orange crack and lit up.

"They're looking at her as if she's their god," Denise whispered to Toby.

He nodded slightly, too entranced by the little creature's weird reaction to immediately reply her.

Jessie dragged in deep of the crack fumes and then, walking along the line of cages, she blew the white smoke at them all, taking her time to refill her lungs between exhalations.

The smoke calmed the animals for a while, and then suddenly they began flinging themselves at the bars with resumed violence.

"Total addiction," Max explained. "A vicious cycle; they're angry when they get the drug, and angry when they don't have any of it." Then he pulled cubes of Agent Orange from his pockets and retracing Jessie's route, dropped one in each cage, upon which the rats, rabbits, and guinea pigs immediately quit their raging and squealing and began eating the drug.

"And it'll just make them more angry," Jessie said. "I sometime shudder at the thought of what they'll do to me, if they ever got out when I was getting high."

"I don't even wanna think about that," Denise told her, then she gave Toby a meaningful stare that said, "I've had more than enough of this freak show; let's leave at once."

Toby who felt exactly the same way, nodded at Max. "Okay, dude where's our consignment?"

Max gestured back towards the living room. "Out there. I make a point of storing all the completed stuff as far away from my test animals as possible, because they can smell it and smelling it makes them even more enraged than normal."

Not even bothering to consider how Max's caged animals would behave when in such a state, Toby and Denise followed the chemist and his crack-addict girlfriend back to the living room to collect the drugs they were going to sell this weekend.

CHAPTER 4

"It was great to see Tony and Lynn again after all this while," Gary Bentley told his wife Charlotte as he drove them back home from meeting up with their old friends. Gary and Charlotte lived outside Elkins, West Virginia, up near the ranger station where Gary worked as a forest ranger.

"Lynn's looking fat," Charlotte said. "I asked her if she was pregnant, and she denied it."

Gary laughed at that. "Maybe she ain't then." Then he laughed. "She's too old for another baby anyway. Just like you!"

Forest ranger Gary Bentley winked at the scandalized expression on his wife's face at that comment. He felt good. He wasn't really one for town life, preferring the green freedom of the natural countryside, but Seeing Tony and Lynn, who were just passing through on their way south to Tennessee, had been brought back lots of great memories of when they'd all been kids together.

But, nah, Tony can keep his high-pressure executive life, Gary thought, stroking his lightly-bearded chin as he steered the family sedan along the mountain roads. *Here in the countryside is the life for me, with just the forest trees and the wildlife critters.*

Charlotte reached up to the dashboard and turned the car radio on.

"... state police are still trying to track down the source of the new designer narcotic called Agent Orange, which has now begun to spread into the states of Ohio and Pennsylvania too. A police spokesman has confirmed that the source of the drug seems to be in Barbour or Randolph counties, but that they've so far been unable to pinpoint the exact location of the manufacturing . . ."

After checking that the highway was empty of oncoming traffic, Gary grimaced over at his wife. They both had harrowing memories where Agent Orange was concerned; all of which concerned a now dead raccoon. "Honey, please change the station," Gary pleaded. "Right now, I'm feeling too good to have to listen to that crap."

Grimacing too, Charlotte switched channels.

". . . And in Zanesville, Ohio, there's been an animal abduction, or maybe we should call it a croc-napping. Bill, a 600 pound Nile crocodile disappeared from the Exotic Wonders Animal Clinic where he'd been taken for medical treatment . . ."

This time Gary didn't bother discussing matters with Charlotte. He quickly took his right hand off the steering wheel and tapped the button to change the radio station again.

"Hey, I was listening to that!" Charlotte immediately protested, as Gary tuned into a college rock station.

Gary smiled at her, but didn't say anything. Charlotte had a soft spot for animals. Gary was in the mood to get into Charlotte's own soft spot tonight and didn't need for her to start moping over a missing crocodile.

Maybe Charlotte was in a lovemaking mood also, because she didn't fight to get the animal news back. Rather, she relaxed back in her seat, and began tapping her feet to the beat of the songs while her husband steered them closer to home through the lush green walls of West Virginian forest.

Gary Bentley smiled to himself. Now that that little news crisis had been averted, he looked forward to a nice romantic evening with Charlotte.

CHAPTER 5

The Pollak brother's black van was now deep in West Virginia. The mountain highway they were riding on was nice and scenic, but neither of the two men in the van were paying much attention to the countryside.

"... At the moment there's no leads as to the thieves' identity, but security at the animal clinic are currently reviewing their CCTV footage and hope to be able to recover Bill the crocodile from his kidnappers very soon. Meanwhile, local law enforcement say—"

Walt switched off the radio.

"Hey, what you do that for?" Jake asked from the van's shotgun seat.

Walt took his eyes off of the highway for a moment. "I know you wanna keep up with developments in the case, but that newscaster was starting to annoy me. The way they're slanting it, you'd think we'd abducted the fucking president."

Jake nodded. "Yeah, it does sound like they're expecting us to send them a damn ransom note."

"It's 'cos there's nothing else of interest happening today," Walt added, with his eyes firmly back on the road now. "There's no human kidnappings, or serial killer arrests . . . no terrorist bombings or major traffic pileups with good body counts, so . . . Bill the croc is becoming a celebrity."

Jake wiped sweat off of his brow. "The sooner we deliver the lizard to Johnson, the better."

Walt nodded. "Yeah, yeah. Let him take the heat. But really, we ain't got nothing to worry about. Tom already texted us to let us know they've no evidence linking us to the snatch, the CCTV just shows two ski-masked guys who could be anyone. So, we're in the clear there."

"Yeah, so long as the cops don't pull us over and enquire what we've got in the back, we're fine."

Walt glanced over at Jake again and frowned. "Only thing I worried about now is Johnson refusing to pay our increased asking price. 'Cos, if he wants to, he can bluff us. If he bluffs us, we've no other options. We can't keep the damn croc in a swimming pool somewhere until we find another buyer. It's too damn big."

Jake gestured into the back of the van and nodded. "Yeah. I'm actually wondering where Johnson is gonna keep Bill—he's twice as big as the man expected him to be."

Walt shrugged. "His problem, not ours. He must've have heard the news by now, so hopefully he'll know what to expect where Bill's size is concerned."

Jake waited till they'd passed a truck approaching them, and then said, "Hey, bro, why don't I call Johnson now? Let him know we want some more money."

Walt mused on that for a while, rolled past two more cars and then nodded. "Alright, that's a good idea. But set it up easy. Say the extra is for expense—"

A loud thumping in the back of the van interrupted their discussion.

"Fuck was that?" Walt asked as the van shook again.

Jake nervously peeked into the back of the van and then shook his head at his brother. "Bill's waking up," he said, as the van shook again.

Walt sighed. "Dammit, I knew the tranks wouldn't do the job for long." He nodded down at the bag that lay between them on the front seat. "Better give Bill another dose of sleep aids before he's awake enough to make a nuisance of himself."

Jake nodded and rummaged in the bag for the tranquilizer gun.

CHAPTER 6

Things were shaping up to be an interesting evening.

Also driving in that picturesque area of the West Virginian countryside at that very time were Toby Morales and Denise Higgins, both of whom were riding in Toby's blue Volkswagen. The couple had the windows down and the stereo cranked up.

Toby and Denise were heading up to the Sleepaway Campground, where they had a couple of drug deliveries to make to camper customers. And Toby was also delivering a large package of chicken for a barbecue.

"I like being out in the countryside," Denise said after a while of watching the trees float past them. "It's so relaxing. Don't you agree, baby?"

The rock music was playing so loud that Toby couldn't make out what his girlfriend was saying. He kept on nodding to the music, with his eyes on the road and his thoughts on the fifty grand's worth of Agent Orange he had in the trunk of his ride.

Denise was smoking a joint and was quite high by that point. The joint naturally made Toby nervous. He understood that constantly flirting with disaster was part of a drug dealer's life, but he still couldn't get used to it. Toby had been in prison twice, once for dealing and the second time for arson, and he had no desire to be locked away again.

"Hey, put that joint out," he told Denise, taking his eyes off of the road for a moment to stare at her ecstatic face and glazed eyes.

The music was of course too loud for Denise to hear him. "What?" she asked loudly.

Toby wanted to snap at her, but decided against it. If he pissed her off, she'd start sulking and if she started sulking, she'd ruin his weekend. She'd still insist on his fucking her though—girl couldn't do without sex—but she'd keep sulking each time he wasn't actively humping her. From experience, Toby could do without the hassle; and the exhaustion that would naturally result from the endless bouts of sex required to keep Denise happy in that condition.

So instead of barking at her, Toby reached over and turned down the car stereo.

"Hey, leave it!" Denise protested as the music seemed to die away. "I like his voice."

"How do you feel about going to jail, baby?" Toby asked sweetly.

Denise tugged on the ends of her black hair and frowned. "What the hell are you talking about?"

Toby adjusted the steering wheel, then looked at her again. "I'm asking 'cos that's where we'll both be heading if the cops pull us over and catch you with that joint in your hand." He grimaced. "Not to mention the other joints you've got in your bag and all the shit I've got stuffed in the trunk."

Denise thought for a moment, then flung her joint out of the car window.

Their car sped away and Toby gaped at her. After a while she gaped back at him. "What's the matter? I thought you wanted me to get rid of it."

He managed to control himself. "Honey, I did, but you were supposed to put it out first. Are you trying to start a forest fire?" Toby had a sudden vision of an army of forest rangers descending on him along with the DEA guys, and dragging him off to a cold slimy cell, where he'd be sentenced to remain till God had mercy on him and let him die.

But the marijuana made Denise oblivious to his concerns. "Stop worrying. It's the middle of summer. The trees are too green to burn. Plus, it rained last night.

"Oh, yeah? Tell that to the forest rangers."

At the moment a police cruiser drove past them, and, imagining that they'd seen Denise ditch the joint, Toby instinctively stiffened.

Because that would be a double offence; both using drugs and trying to set the forest on fire. And if one of them decided he wanted to see what Toby had in his trunk . . .

So, Toby held his breath and a sense of dread possessed and chilled him, but neither officer in the police SUV even glanced into his car at he and Denise as it passed them and then sped off into the distance.

"See, I told you to stop worrying," Denise repeated as the police cruiser became a distant black and white dot.

Toby was about to retort to this, but before he could, Denise asked: "What're you so bothered about anyway? Those little critters Max has in his lab? You seem all worked up this evening, is why I'm asking."

Toby had forgotten about Max's lab rats. Now their little orange eyes haunted him. "Oh, baby, those were damn creepy," he said with a shudder.

CHAPTER 7

Walt and Jake Pollak were in more than a little trouble. Yes, they had located the tranquilizer darts in the bag, but Jake was having trouble getting the gun loaded up in the cramped space of the front of the van, with Bill the crocodile growing more and more active in the rear of the vehicle.

"For God's sake, put that thing back to sleep!" Walt groaned at his brother. "Once it starts throwing itself around in there, there's no telling what else is gonna happen."

"Yeah, sure." Jake gulped, now very thankful that a wall of steel separated he and his brother from the reptile in the rear. Even with that, the creature's reptilian musk seemingly oozed out of the three-inch-square observation hole in the metal screen.

Bill seemed fully awake now, and Jake figured the huge beast could smell he and his brother here in the front, and that it remembered them from the Ohio animal clinic. And looking into the crocodile's expressionless yellow eyes as it eyed him through the square opening in the steel separation between the front and rear of the vehicle, Jake got the impression that their passenger was mad, angry at them for removing it from its comfy lodgings at the animal hotel where a free goat lunch had even been provided. Now it was stuck in the cramped rear of their vehicle, hardly unable to maneuver itself in any direction at all (to fit the animal in the van, they'd had to fold his tail forward next to his body) and most likely quite uncomfortable.

So, yes, maybe Bill the crocodile does have a valid basis for a grudge against us, Jake thought nervously as he watched the crocodile shift restlessly and continue to bump its head and body against the sides of its metal confinement. *It's pissed off 'cos of the tranks we hit it with and wants some damn payback. Or maybe, it's just hungry, and figures we'll make it a nice snack before it gets another goat tossed its way. Damn thing most likely imagines we're returning it home to the zoo anyway.*

Bill opened his jaws wide and hissed at them. After a scary peek down that long row of teeth, Jake got back to loading up his tranquiller gun.

"Hey, just calm down in there," he told the crocodile. "You'll be able to resume dreaming in a little bit."

"The hell's taking you so long to get that air rifle loaded anyway?" Walt asked, throwing him a dark look. "It ain't like this is the first time you've ever done this."

Jake rolled his eyes. "Yeah, but that damn crocodile is making my hands shake with fear, that's why." He pointed down at the floor, at the remains of two shattered tranquilizer darts, their contents spilled away on the foot mat.

"Relax, bro," Walt said, while keeping his eyes on the road. "Our passenger might be a big boy, but he can't get to us, no matter what happens. Flesh against steel is no competition; no way is big Bill in back there breaking through to us here in the front." Then he glanced away from the road again and stared coldly at his brother. "So, please, get your damn shit together and shoot a couple of darts into Bill's mouth, before he really gets pissed with us."

Jake nodded. Walt returned his attention to the road. "Just calm down, bro. Just calm down. We're almost out of the woods here. Once we make it to Elkins, we'll hand the animal over to Johnson and get paid."

Walt's voice was calm and factual, but Jake still thought he detected an element of fright in it.

He picked a fresh tranquilizer dart out from their box and attempted to load it into the rifle again. Almost as if he knew what was happening up front, Bill chose that exact moment to throw himself sideways against the side of the van.

The impact was so forceful that Jake again lost his grip on both the dart and the gun. The dart went flying out through the window, and

Jake barely escaped getting the muzzle of the rifle stuck deep in his right eye.

"Shit!" he growled in anger.

He thought Walt would chew him out for losing yet another precious dart, but Walt didn't. Walt had problems of his own. He was fighting to maintain control of the van as Bill now began throwing himself left and right against its walls.

"Please, li'l bro, get that damn rifle loaded up and put that damn animal back to sleep," Walt said through clenched teeth. "If you don't do it soon, we're gonna lose our investment and go to jail to boot."

Jake almost laughed at the request. Tough Walt looked like he was about to cry. Whether from fright, or from fear of lost profits, Jake couldn't tell. It was a sight to see though.

Jake got out a fresh dart from the box and once more tried fitting it into the dart gun, while Bill the crocodile violently wobbled their van along the highway.

CHAPTER 8

"I really wish we didn't have to work with Max," Denise said after Toby been driving in silence for a while. "That guy is super creepy."

"Yeah, yeah, baby, but it's only for a short while," Toby said. "We've discussed this before. We stay with Max for just as long as it takes to get a good nest egg, and then we'll ditch him and hit the highway for greener pastures. I'm thinking we should head to California."

Denise nodded. "That's fine with me. I'm sick of small-town life. About the only good thing here is the dope."

Which won't last very long with the kind of attention Agent Orange is getting now, Toby thought with a grimace. *If only Max understood how important it is to neutralize whatever chemicals he's got in there that are driving people crazy, we'd be riding the damn gravy train.*

Then Toby felt a touch in his lap. Oops!

He glanced down, and saw that Denise had a firm hold of his penis through his pants. She moved closer to him and began massaging his manhood.

"You seem very stressed up, baby," Denise purred. "A handjob will relax you just fine."

"Honey, we've got fifty grand's worth of 'Orange' in the trunk."

But Denise only giggled. "Oh, the cops'll never notice it, the way I packed the it in with those chicken meat your lezzie friend wants for tomorrow's barbeque."

Caught between his worries and the sweet feeling of her fingers playing in his lap, Toby couldn't reply her.

It had been a last moment's decision to stash the Agent Orange shipment amongst Dean's chicken barbeque meat. The drug package had an airtight seal on it, so there was no chance of the chicken dripping on it, and it also had a similar look to the chicken packages, because Max had used foam trays similar to those used in butcher shops to sell meat. These trays had the product portioned out and shrink-wrapped.

Toby couldn't disagree that in with the chickens was the perfect hiding place for their drug stash, and yet, as his penis grew harder and harder in his pants because of Denise's manipulations, he also couldn't shake the feeling that suddenly came over him, a repeat of the dread anticipation that he'd felt when the police cruiser had shown in his rearview mirrors, that the elements of this pleasant evening were developing into a disaster.

He had no idea how correct he was.

Cars passed them and Denise kept working on Toby's penis while he drove.

Judging from familiar landmarks all around, the Sleepaway Campground turnoff was about three miles away now, and Toby knew that the first thing he was gonna do once they reached the campground parking lot was dump Denise in the backseat and fuck her hard, which was clearly the real reason she was getting him worked up.

But then, to have better access to his cock, Denise pulled his zipper down. She did so forcefully, however, which resulted in the zipper snagging halfway, so she worked it back up to get past the obstruction. But, still being partly stoned, Denise once more wasn't careful about what she was doing. She yanked up the zipper just as forcefully as she'd pulled it down, which unfortunately resulted in the teeth of the zipper capturing some of Toby's pubic hair as it closed up again.

"Ouch!" Toby howled at the sudden pain in his crotch, and then lost control of the car, both reflexly stomping down on the gas pedal and jerking the steering wheel to the left as a long black van was approaching them in the opposite lane.

"Shit!" Toby shouted as his car skidded across the double yellow line towards the oncoming van.

Worse still, the oncoming van also seemed to be out of control. The guy behind the wheel seemed to be fighting a battle to keep the vehicle moving in a straight line.

"What the matter, honey?" Denise asked, finally paying attention to the road as Toby's car swerved towards the black van, whose driver was now desperately trying to get out of their way on the small mountain road.

CHAPTER 9

Try hard as he might, Jake hadn't been able to get the tranquilizer gun loaded. Each time he'd almost gotten it done, Bill would slam into the van from yet another awkward angle and either the gun or the dart would go flying. Several times, Jake himself had gone flying, flung through the air by the violence of the crocodile's impact with the van, and either slamming into his brother; or once, nearly being flung out of the window on his side of the van.

Walt was almost going out of his mind just trying to keep their van on the road, as each violent jerk by their reptile prisoner threatened to knock it off the road and into the forest.

Neither brother's state of mind was helped at all by the fact that they could hear the enraged beast in the back attempting to bite his way through the metal wall that separated the van's front and rear compartments.

Yeah, sure, Walt thought as he fought to keep the van level on their side of the highway. *Yeah, I just told Jake that in a combat between flesh and steel, steel always wins, but what if I'm wrong. I'm not saying I believe Bill can actually bite through solid steel plate, but he might be able to knock the plate down flat and reach us that way. Either way, the end result is gonna be the same; me and my bro are both gonna be deader than dead fish.*

A couple drove past them in an SUV. They seemed to be arguing, which was why they'd not noticed the odd way the van was behaving.

"Pull over to the side," Jake suddenly said.

Walt looked at Jake like he was mad. "What?"

Almost as if he too was surprised by Jake's suggestion, Bill stopped thrashing about at that exact moment. The brothers could hear the

31

crocodile breathing in the back though, loud jagged breaths as if he was either exhausted or excited.

Jake, who now had a desperately frightened look on his face, nodded at Walt. "Yeah, I'm serious, bro. Pull the van over to the roadside and park." Walt saw he was holding up a pair of tranquiller darts. "These are the last two," he explained in a harassed voice. "If we lose them too, we'll be in deep shit. So, park the van and let me load up and put Bill to sleep again, before those cops that passed us earlier drive back this way."

Walt felt intense relief. Jake had come up with the perfect solution, one which he himself might have come up with, assuming he'd not been so worried about them being stopped.

"Yeah," he agreed as Bill resumed moving about again in the back. "Just let's reach a stretch of road that ain't as thickly wooded as this, so we don't obstruct traffic."

So, they drove on. And that was when both men spotted the dark blue sedan in the oncoming lane lose control and veer across the road towards them.

***

Walt immediately tried to avoid the oncoming car. He could see that the driver of the car looked as scared as he did; the man was also fighting to control his vehicle. He had a woman in the car with him who was staring open-mouthed at the van as if it was a product of a magic trick.

At first it looked as if disaster would be averted. Walt had a firm grip of the steering wheel, he figured he'd be able to make it past the skidding car without the vehicles making contact. Though panicked, his long years of driving experience had now kicked in. He'd read the danger quickly, evaluated his possible responses to the situation, and adjusted the van's motion in accordance with his mental calculations.

In another situation, the most logical thing to do to avoid the out-of-control car would be to simply drive off the road into the forest, because at this section of the highway the trees weren't so tightly packed together and the forest also began a short distance in from the road. Unfortunately, in this current situation this solution wasn't possible as a recent storm seemed to have eroded the portion of earth right next to the road, leaving several deep ruts. Attempting to drive over those would severely bust up the van's undercarriage.

So, trusting both to fate and to his driving skills, Walt attempted to stay on the blacktop, but keeping as close to its edge as he could.

And it would have worked too. The other driver looked to have gotten his car under control; its rear end was going to straighten out just in time to miss hitting the van.

But then, as if willing the accident to happen, the crocodile in the rear flung himself at the walls again. The impact was so violent this time that it shifted the van sideways, ensuring that a collision occurred. The collision was minor, but Bill's violence also launched Jake across the front of the vehicle yet again, causing him to crash into Walt and block off Walt's vision right when Walt needed to see where he was driving.

Jake also knocked Walt's hands sideways on the steering wheel. Walt lost control of the van, which then swerved across the double yellow line and into the opposite lane. Thankfully, there were no cars approaching either way and total disaster still might have been averted. But, now possibly excited by the commotion he'd caused, Bill began making a complete nuisance of himself in the back of the van, flinging himself back and forth in there and so, unintentionally causing the rear of the van to go into a long skid when Walt slammed on the brakes.

The erosion at the highway's edge was equally as bad on this side as on the other. Long story short, once Jake and Walt's van hit one of those deep ruts, what had begun as a skid quickly became a series of bounces and somersaults, a journey which for the Pollak brothers consisted of the noise of metal separating from metal, and the noise of inflating airbags.

Thankfully, during this portion of their journey, Bill the crocodile was silent, the animal most likely traumatized by being overturned again and again.

Then the van crashed at the base of a large tree and there was silence for a while.

CHAPTER 10

Toby and Denise's car had fared better than the van, even though Toby had no idea what exactly had happened. He'd gotten his car straightened out just in time—he was certain of this—and then, all of a sudden, it had seemed as if something solid had slammed into the side of the van, flinging it sideways towards his car again. His natural reaction had been to twist the steering wheel as far right as he could, while Denise gripped his arm tightly.

However, Toby couldn't get the car straightened out again in time to stop it running off the road. As every road safety commercial about wearing seatbelts that he'd watched in his life flashed before his eyes, he gripped the steering wheel tight, stomped on the brakes, and hoped for the best. Denise was now praying.

Their car bounced over a deep rut at the edge of the road and then plunged into the forest. Fortune smiled on Toby and Denise, because their car missed ramming into any of the trees and instead plunged into a natural gap between them. The depression in the road had both destroyed the vehicle's transmission and also slowed it down, so the blue sedan finally came to rest with just the slightest of bumps.

After saying his own silent prayers thanking God that he was still alive, Toby Morales got out of his car and helped Denise out also. The pair of them stood there, surrounded by trees, in a sort of glade in the middle of the forest.

Denise stood holding Toby tight like she was groggy; most likely from a combo of marijuana and the crash. As far as Toby could see, she wasn't hurt either.

The pair of them stood staring at the car. The blue Volkswagen Jetta was visually wrecked. It wasn't going anywhere from here except to a car repair workshop.

Toby looked back up the avenue of greenery they'd traversed to come to this halt. There was a walk of thirty yards or so back to the highway.

Then Toby remembered the van they'd hit.

What the hell happened to the two guys in the van?

CHAPTER 11

When the loud explosion of white noise ceased ringing in Walt
Pollak's ears, he realized he was still alive.

Walt's perspective was however a little odd. Then, after a few
seconds of wondering why the world seemed different from when he'd
last been in it, he understood what was wrong. He'd been sitting
upright and now he was lying on his side. So, of course the world
looked different.

Then he remembered exactly why he was now lying on his side and
was instantly frightened again. *The out-of-control car . . . the crash . . . that
goddamn gator . . . no goddam crocodile, though it's up to God tell them apart.*

And Jake . . . where's Jake?

A loud groan from beneath him informed him that he was lying on
top of his younger brother.

"You okay, bro?"

"Just fucking get off of me!"

This angry response assured Walt Pollak that aside from some
bleeding cuts on his head, Jake Emery Pollak was right as rain. Which
made Walt review his own physical condition as well and realize that
his guardian angel must be working overtime today, as he was even less
scratched that Jake was.

"Man, we're in deep shit now," Jake said. "We'd better get away
from here before help arrives. And for fuck's sake, Mikey, get off of
me!"

Spurred into motion by Jake's words, Walt stood up off of him.
And then, after untangling themselves from the deflated airbags in the
front of the van, the two brothers climbed up out of the driver's side
door.

They'd come to a halt about five yards in from the highway, which was still deserted at the moment.

"I wonder what happened to the other car," Jake said, while gazing at the deep trench their van had sliced into the forest floor, which, from the looks of things, had included uprooting several saplings. Then he looked up and down their stretch of road. "I don't seen no sign of them anywhere."

"Maybe they got scared and drove off," Walt replied.

However, Walt wasn't really thinking of the car that had caused the accident.

Yes, we really are in deep shit, sir, he thought miserably as he stared at the overturned van. *No wheels, and a stolen croc in the back, which spells a long jail term for us both once the police realize this is the animal that went missing from Ohio this afternoon.*

Though the loss of revenue from selling Bill greatly upset him, Walt thought quickly and pragmatically. *Jake and I had better clear out right now. That way, we'll have a fighting chance to argue in court that someone else both stole our van and stole Bill, and not ourselves.*

"Hey, Jake, let's get our stuff out and make tracks into the woods," he said next, after a quick glance towards the highway, which still revealed the road as empty.

Clearly their luck was holding. Walt didn't really believe in fate or destiny, but he now felt that perhaps this simply wasn't the day for things to go wrong for him.

Then he glanced towards the rear of the van, where Jake stood with a stupefied look on his face like he'd gotten a concussion in the crash.

"Hey, Walt, Bill's gone," Jake said.

It took a few moments for the meaning of that statement to filter into Walt Pollak's consciousness, and then he stared in surprise at his brother. "What the fuck do you mean, Bill is gone?"

Jake shrugged. "Exactly that, man. The crocodile is no longer in the back of the van."

Still in disbelief, Walt hurried over to the rear of the van and looked into it himself. The crash had burst open the rear doors and . . . yep, just as his brother had informed him, there was no crocodile in sight.

"Where the hell can he have gotten to?" Walt said.

"We'd better just get away from here before someone comes," Jake said.

But Walt, who'd just realized that the crocodile's disappearance had gotten them both out of a robbery rap, shook his head. "No need to run now. No Bill in our van means no evidence. And we didn't cause the car crash either. So, we'll just remain here and play the victim."

Jake nodded, taking this in. "So, what do we do about Bill then? That's a lot of cash to let walk away like that."

Walt sighed. "Better than going to jail for." Then he brightened up a bit and said, "Listen, wait right here, while I head into the woods for a quick look around. I wanna see if I can tell what direction our crocodile went."

"I don't notice any croc tracks around here," Jake said. "How you gonna find him?"

Walt smirked at his brother. "You forget I'm an ex-forest ranger. I'm more used to tracking animals than you are. For one thing, rest assured that a gator or croc will naturally seek out a body of water— that's its natural habitat."

Walt ran towards the front of the van and quickly lowered himself back inside the vehicle. He opened up the glove compartment, got out his revolver and then climbed back out. He didn't want to have to kill Bill, but if it came down to that, then the damn croc was history.

"Okay, keep watch for a few minutes while I go have a look-see where our missing paycheck's gotten to," he told his brother. "Anybody ask where I am, tell them I must've gotten groggy and staggered off."

But Jake shook his head. "No, I'll say you went off to do number two. No one's ever in a hurry to find a guy who's taking a shit."

Laughing at the joke, Walt hurried off into the woods to look for Bill.

CHAPTER 12

"We'd better go give those guys a hand," Toby said.

"Yeah," Denise quickly agreed. " 'Specially since it's our fault an' all."

She and Toby set off walking towards the highway, but just as they reached the point where they'd run in off the road, Denise pulled Toby back.

"No need to go help them," she said. "Someone's stopping."

Toby watched as a vehicle pulled up by the roadside, up where the van seemed to have crashed into the forest.

CHAPTER 13

Charlotte Bentley noticed the overturned van before her husband did. Then, once she'd pointed it out to him, Gary slowed their car and reversed. Then while Charlotte was still taking in the strange sight of the black van with its wheels pointing outwards at the road, her husband had already leapt down and was hurrying around the front of their car towards the crashed vehicle.

Watching him charge off like that, Charlotte felt a surge off admiration. Yes, that was her man. Gary Bentley was a man of action, which if he was to be honest, he really didn't see enough of as a forest ranger.

Maybe he'd have been better suited in the Army or Marines, Charlotte thought with a rush of warmth, *but no, he's too tied to the forest and its wildlife. He loves the woodlands and is dedicated to protecting them and the little critters that inhabit them.*

Charlotte got out of the car and walked over

CHAPTER 14

The good thing about crocs and gators is that they can't ambush you.

This fact was uppermost in Walt Pollak's thoughts as, gun in hand, he pushed his way deeper through the forest leaves.

On land, both large species of reptiles were clumsy, if still very dangerous.

But once they get ya into the water, watch out . . .

But, gun in hand or not, Walt had no intention of ever swimming in crocodile- or gator-infested waters, so this latter detail didn't worry him too much.

Since leaving his brother by their crashed van, Walt had found several of Bill's footprints. In each case the prints led away from the highway. Once, he'd also come across a rut that he supposed had been made by Bill's tail.

Despite the unlikelihood of croc-ambush, however, Walt felt edgy. He flinched each time the wind rustled the leaves near his ears. Once, he almost peed himself when a snake slithered down a tree on his right. It didn't matter what people said about how nice the woods were; being alone in them was creepy.

Alright, time to head back, Walt decided on finding two more large reptile footprints. These pair were aimed in the same direction as the previous ones, which meant Bill was walking in a straight line. Walt didn't know if this was because the crocodile was groggy or because it could smell water nearby; or even simply because the ground here had a descending slope which made 'forward' the natural direction in which to proceed.

It didn't matter. What did matter now was for Walt to work out where he was currently. And so, he got out his phone and opened up Google Maps.

Okay, so I'm here up on Laurel Mountain and bingo. As far as Walt could tell from Google Maps, he was standing about three hundred yards away from Teter Creek, which, eventually fed downhill into Teter Creek Lake.

Walt Pollak smiled to himself. Satisfied that he now knew where he'd find Bill when he was ready to trap him again, Walt concealed his pistol beneath his tee shirt and headed back towards the highway again.

CHAPTER 15

Though the crash was quite an elaborate one, there didn't seem to be any loss of life. By the time Charlotte reached the overturned van, Gary was interviewing a tall man, while another, shorter man was just stepping out of the forest.

"Call of nature," the shorter man explained when he reached the three of them. "When the van crashed it felt like my insides all got scrambled up at once."

"Your brother told me as much," Gary said. "So, you're sure it's just the two of you guys? No casualties you need an ambulance for?"

The man who'd emerged from the bushes shook his head. "Nah, we just need a tow truck, though Jake may need some stitches too for those cuts on his head."

Gary nodded and got out his cellphone. Charlotte listened to him make his emergency call and then walked off towards the rear of the van.

The rear door had come open during the crash. Charlotte wondered where they'd been headed. She leaned over and peeked into the rear, but it was empty. It did however have a slightly musky animal smell. Or was that simply her imagination?

Charlotte decided that it might be; she loved animals, particularly all the little woodland critters. She was so fond of animals like raccoons and squirrels that in the earlier years of her marriage to Gary, it had led to quarrels between them.

The musky smell coming from the rear of the van wasn't one that Charlotte was familiar with and so she quickly dismissed it from her mind.

Charlotte straightened up and walked a short distance from the van, over to where the ground wasn't as smashed up. Her intent was to sit down on a tree stump while Gary attended to the crash victims.

But while sitting, Charlotte's gaze happened to fall on a strange-looking object. She picked it up to see better. The object was a tooth; one which, from the look of things, had recently been in an animal's mouth; the point of extraction was still wet and bloody. The tooth was long and sharp, and its owner had clearly been quite a large animal.

Charlotte racked her brain and tried to imagine the animal it had come from. Something the size of a bear at least. She tried to visualize ursine dentition, trying to fit the tooth into that dental model.

She had no luck with this, and when she looked up and noticed that other cars had stopped to help the accident victims, Charlotte slipped the large tooth in her pocket to ponder on later.

"I think the other car must've driven off," Jake was saying, as Charlotte once more joined her husband beside he and his brother.

"Yeah," Jake's brother agreed. "I don't think they even realized our car crashed."

It was an innocent enough statement, but for some reason it rang bells of falsehood in Charlotte's ears.

CHAPTER 16

"Alright, now that we're sure they're not dead, let's get the hell out of here," Toby finally told Denise.

The pair of them had stood behind a tree, watching the accident site up ahead for almost thirty minutes, while more cars pulled to the side to render assistance and then finally a tow truck showed up. The fact that there was no ambulance was a relief to Toby and Denise.

"Oh, I'd really never forgive myself if someone died because I wanted to fuck you," Denise said.

"You almost sound serious about that," Toby joked.

"I am fucking serious," she retorted, then was silent for a while.

"So, what do we do now?" Denise asked after that pause, "It's getting kinda late. Gonna be dark soon. Do we walk up the road and introduce ourselves, and tell them we need help too?"

Toby shook his head. "Easy route to the county lockup. You're forgetting the drugs in our car."

Denise thought on that for a second or two. "We can hide the Agent Orange and come back for it later."

But Toby shook his head again. "Nah, we're almost at the Sleepaway Campground turnoff now. What I suggest we do is, leave the car here, take the drugs and head down to the camp. We can attend to the car later." He stared at his wristwatch, made a mental calculation, and then got out his cellphone and tapped off a text message.

"Who you texting?" Denise asked.

"Dean and Monique. I wanna know if they've arrived at the camp yet. The sooner we hand their chicken over to them, the better."

"We can't leave the meat in the trunk," Denise said. "It'll spoil in the heat."

Toby nodded. "Yeah, we'll carry it with us. It's great camouflage."

They walked back towards their own crashed vehicle, which they both now realized was so deep in the woods that no one could see it from the road. And seeing as not a single person had walked down this way to look for them and their vehicle, apparently the men in the van hadn't mentioned them either.

The reply to Toby's text came in just as they reached the blue Jetta.

Toby read through it and nodded to Denise, who was now sitting on the hood of the car with her arms folded around her drawn-up legs. "They'll be here in about an hour. Monique's younger sister got sick and had to be taken to the doctor. But she's okay now."

Denise nodded and leapt down from the hood. "Okay, let's head out then. It'll be nightfall in half an hour."

Toby opened the hood and they offloaded their bags of clothes along with the plastic shopping bag that contained Dean's raw chicken and the Agent Orange.

The frozen chicken had thawed from the warmth in the trunk and Toby winced at the smell, which resulted in Denise handing him her cellphone to hold and carrying the bag of food herself.

With that settled, they removed their other valuables from the car and headed into the woods, away from the highway. From their point of setting out, the Sleepaway Campground was about five hundred yards off.

CHAPTER 17

Guided by instinct, Bill the Nile crocodile just kept on walking. He knew there was water nearby and he intended to find that water. In many ways, this place was similar to his natural African habitat and he sensed there was flowing water very close by.

Bill was a creature with a large body but a small brain. But he had also a large appetite. In addition to needing water, he had also begun feeling hungry.

Those two humans had disrupted his last feeding, and as much as an unintelligent beast could, Bill felt anger towards them both.

CHAPTER 18

"Those two struck me as being extremely fishy," Charlotte said as Gary drove them both away from the site of the accident.

Gary looked away from the road for a moment. He'd been having exactly the same feeling about the Pollak brothers. Something was off about the pair, that was for sure, but everything about them had seemed legit, so he'd not made any side comments about them to Chomski and Swick the two policemen who'd arrived at the site along with the tow truck.

"How do you mean, 'fishy,' darling?" Gary asked.

Charlotte shrugged. "It wasn't something I could put a finger on, or said specifically. But they both had the behavior of guys who'd gotten away with something and were desperate not to draw attention to themselves."

While her husband both mused on this and made a turning off of the main highway onto the road that led to their cabin, Charlotte added: "If I was to state it any better, I'd do so by asking this question: Why in the world would anyone lie about someone else *not* causing an accident they'd been involved in?" She ran fingers through her hair and looked confused. "Because, honey, that's what it seemed to me that they were doing. Like they were desperate not to have anyone else interviewed about the accident but themselves."

Gary nodded and felt bothered. He'd not given it that much thought at the time, but maybe, just maybe, Charlotte had a point there.

"Well, it's out of our hands now," he told her with a smile, as their car rolled onto their gravel driveway. "Thankfully, no one got injured or killed in the crash." He shrugged. "If the police find anything suspicious about those two brothers, they'll know where to find 'em."

CHAPTER 19

There were several cars in the parking lot of the Sleepaway Campground when Toby and Denise arrived there.

By now Toby had gotten over his aversion to the raw chicken smell that was coming from the plastic shopping bag and had accepted it from Denise, largely so she could light up a joint. After the way she'd disposed of her last joint out of his car window, Toby had had his reservations about her smoking in the woods, but there was no doubt that the marijuana made their trudge through the woods less boring.

It however had gotten Denise seeing things.

"Hey, ain't that a gator over there?" Denise had asked at one point.

Toby had looked over in the direction she'd indicated, but had seen nothing; which had of course made him look strangely at his girlfriend.

"Oh, forget it then," Denise said. "Must be the grass making me see things."

Toby let it go at that, but still he felt uneasy afterwards. When she'd been pointing out the supposed gator, Denise hadn't sounded stoned or playful. She'd sounded dead serious.

Now that they'd reached the parking lot, they had a choice of options. Seeing as they hadn't brought along any camping gear with them, they would clearly be rooming in one of the log cabins erected on the opposite side of the river that ran through the campground. There were two cabins opposite them now, assuming they walked the hundred or so yards to the river bank, where there was a bridge to the other side.

"So, here or there?" Denise asked, gesturing first at the nearby cabins, and then gesturing to her right, referring to the other handful wooden cabins peppering the landscape about a quarter mile down the river.

Toby frowned. "There. You know how Dean is about not camping near the parking lot because the woods around here tend to get more crowded with people." He checked his watch again. "The girl should get here quickly and relieve me of this chicken burden."

Denise laughed at that. "Don't be in such a rush. Now that we don't have our car, where you gonna hide the Agent Orange once you've handed Dean her chicken wings and thighs and whatever?"

"I'll secure it between the cheeks of your ass, baby. Lots of hiding space in there."

Denise laughed and dropped the remnants of their joint on the gravel parking area the two were standing in. Toby didn't comment. The nearest trees were fifty yards off and also, currently there was no breeze blowing that could carry a spark over to them.

He nodded down the woodland trail that led west. "We'd better start hiking then."

Their trip along the trail was made both comfortable and uncomfortable by Denise's insistence on walking directly in front of Toby and every now and then, pausing to rub her buttocks against his crotch. They'd left the parking area well behind now and there were no cars anywhere in sight, and soon Toby had an erection again of the same stiffness as he'd gotten in their car on the way over. He understood that Denise wanted to be fucked, and were it not for the faint possibility that a group of campers (or, God forbid, maybe even a park ranger) might stride along this way at any moment, Toby would have thrown Denise down onto the short grass at the trail's edge and fucked her brains out.

But for the moment at least, reason got the better of his libido and he resolved to control his lusty urges until they reached the western section of the river bank, where there was certain to be nobody around. It was getting dark now anyway.

And this was when Denise suddenly said, "Hey, there's that gator again! I knew I wasn't seeing things!"

Toby gave a start and then peered into the woods in the direction Denise was pointing. Once again however, he saw nothing. He saw no gator lurking in there amongst the trees. Toby didn't even notice any rustling leaves to indicate that a gator might left the spot Denise was pointing at right before he'd looked that way.

Once again Denise looked perplexed, and then told him to forget it, that she must've been mistaken.

Once again (now in part motivated by his intense desire to fuck Denise) Toby nodded his agreement, and yet, he once more felt an intense disquiet, because Denise had again sounded dead serious about seeing a gator in the nearby woods.

It was very curious and might really have puzzled him if he'd not been so horny. *Besides, there are no gators in West Virginia…to far north,* he briefly mused.

So, they proceeded on. After that slight distraction, Denise resumed her mincing walk along the trail, with each backing up to rub her ass against Toby's crotch making him pray fervently that he didn't come in his pants before they reached the riverbank.

His prayers were answered. All of a sudden, they reached the place where the trail forked in two, and a minute later, Toby was rewarded with the sight of flowing water, with a bridge crossing over it. No river had never looked that good to Toby Morales before, and as he approached it, he unzipped his pants in anticipation of the sex to follow.

"Ah yeah, so here we are," he said, when they were twenty yards from the bridge.

As expected, there was no one else in sight. He dropped the bag of chicken and drugs on a grassy ledge and grabbed hold of Denise.

She turned around and laughed when she saw that he'd already freed his erection. "Wow, someone sure is happy to see me today," she laughed in delight.

Toby grunted a sort-of reply to that and then pushed Denise down to her knees and stuck his stiff penis in her mouth. Denise had primed him like a pump and almost immediately he was coming, filling her mouth with sperm. In fact, he ejaculated so much that Denise pulled her mouth off of his cock and milked the rest of the semen from him with her hands.

"Wow, that was quite a load," she laughed as the sperm ran out of the corners of her mouth.

"Baby, you've got my balls working overtime," Toby said in a relieved voice. It felt as if the world's greatest burden had just been lifted off of his shoulders.

Denise fell back from her kneeling position to a sitting one, and then, like she normally did after fellating Toby, she began licking the spilled semen off of her hands. At first, she looked really pleased with herself, but then, her facial expression turned to one of fright.

"Oh my God no, Toby," she gasped. "I wasn't seeing things. It's that gator again!"

Toby was facing Denise and so, whatever she was looking at was behind him. He was also in a relaxed frame of mind after his orgasm, and so it took a while for the impact of her words to really sink in. And that really only happened because the look of fright on Denise's face didn't vanish and become good-natured mockery at the joke she'd sprung on him. No, just like before, she seemed dead serious. She'd even stopped licking the sperm off of her hands.

So, Toby slowly turned around to see what had Denise so spooked.

This time Toby saw that Denise was correct. There was a giant alligator standing behind them, bigger than any alligator Toby had ever seen in his life.

In fact, if he hadn't known better, Toby would have thought the creature wasn't a gator at all, but was really a crocodile.

"You were right all along," he gasped as he scrambled over to Denise's side while hastily zipping up his pants.

Together, they gaped in horror at the giant reptile. The river monster was about ten yards away from them and seemed to be making up its mind whether to attack them or not. In the fading light it was impossible to tell if it had come out of the river or not. They couldn't make out any wetness on its body.

"I'm confused," Denise said. "How long has that thing been following us for?"

"Maybe since we left the car," Toby replied her. Then, after shaking his head as if to clear it, he added: "No, that don't make sense. Or yes, maybe it does make sense. But what doesn't make sense, is what a gator is doing around these parts in the first place. They aren't native to this area."

At that very moment, the supposed alligator stepped forward and they instinctively stepped backward.

"Don't you think we should get away from here?" Denise asked when the 'gator' opened its mouth and bellowed at them.

"No, hold on a bit."

"But why?" Denise asked, gripping on to his arm in her fright.

"We can't leave without the Agent Orange," Toby patiently reminded her. "That's fifty thousand dollars' worth of 'Orange' in that shopping bag. We can't run the risk of someone else finding it if we run off." He leaned over and kissed Denise's hair. He felt emboldened because the gator was still making no attempt to cross to them, besides which he had already determined that from its slow thread they could easily outrun the beast if it came at them. The problem now was that the gator was too near to the bag containing the raw chicken and Agent Orange for Toby to risk going to retrieve the bag from where he'd dropped it.

And then the improbable and seemingly unthinkable happened. With a sideways swerve of its giant snout, the gator snapped up the plastic bag containing the chicken and Agent Orange.

And that was when it hit Toby as to why the alligator has been following himself and Denise all this while. Apparently, it had smelled the thawing chicken flesh in the bag.

Toby now remembered something he read somewhere about how alligators and crocodiles could smell rotten meat up to four miles away. In that regard, they were even better than sharks.

Toby cringed as the gator chomped down on the plastic bag. He didn't give a shit about the chicken; he could always get some more for

Dean. But it would be a total disaster to let fifty thousand dollars' worth of Agent Orange go down the beast's throat.

So, throwing both caution and common sense to the wind, Toby charged at the animal.

"Hey come back!" Denise yelled after him, but he paid no heed to her cry. In seconds, he was at the gator's side, trying to somehow retrieve the drugs from the package that was now clearly on its way down the animal's throat.

Sloping downward to the water, the riverbank was uneven at this point, graded with rocks at different levels, and Toby was standing on a lower elevation than the giant reptile, which made it easier for him to grasp the bag in the 'gator's' mouth, but which would have also made it much easier for the animal to bite his head off, were its powerful jaws not full of chicken.

Toby was still calculating if he could stick his hand into the gator's mouth, when the beast, moving deceptively fast for its size, turned its huge body sideways and swung its tail at him.

The massive tail hit Toby, who, both due to the lower elevation he stood on with relation to the 'gator' and the way he was bent over, took the blow on the hip.

With a yelp of pain Toby was knocked off of his feet and went flying through the air, out of sight among the trees.

Biting her knuckles, and scared to move from where she was, Denise watched the gator completely swallow the package of chicken and drugs.

"Well, there just went fifty thousand dollars of Max's money, she thought coldly, waiting for the gator to return to the river so that she could find Toby and they both could call Max to inform him of the disaster.

She figured they would also need to call wildlife services to come deal with the gator before it hurt anyone at the campground.

Something weird was happening to the animal however. For one thing, it seemed to be getting bigger. And secondly, even in the falling darkness Denise could tell that its formerly yellow eyes now appeared to have a faint orange glow to them, like dimly-powered lamps someone had just turned on.

With a sinking feeling, she recalled the crazy enraged animals in the cages in Max's laboratory, and what he had said about animals having almost no resistance to Agent Orange.

Fuck! she thought, *we've a huge problem here!*

CHAPTER 20

Denise waited and waited for the gator to leave the spot where she and Toby's bags lay. Seeing as night had fallen and darkness ruled the woods now, she needed the flashlight in her bag to enable her to find her boyfriend.

Locating Toby shouldn't be too difficult. Yes, he'd been smacked into the air by the gator's tail, but he couldn't be too far off, could he?

But despite her assurance that Toby had to be somewhere nearby, if inexplicably out of sight, Denise felt rooted in place where she stood. After a while she unfroze sufficiently to move, but still her fear drove her behind the trunk of a large tree. The massiveness of the animal blocking her way was one problem; but the more frightening issue was the bright orange color of its eyes, which now unbelievably shone like electric lamps glued to the sides of its head.

Finally, however, the gator rose to its feet and lumbered off towards the river.

Denise cussed when the animal's seven-foot-long tail crashed down on she and Toby's cellphones, with an instant accompanying crunch of shattering glass and twin bright flickers that died immediately afterwards.

"Shit, there goes our phones!" An intense wave of frustration washed over her. With her cellphone very likely out of commission, she felt cut off from both the world and safety.

Still, extremely aware of the dangerous animal mere yards away from her, she didn't stir from her concealment. She waited until she heard the splash of the gator's body entering the river. After the noise subsided, she dashed over to the bags on the grass. But now she felt extremely worried that Toby hadn't shown up. What the hell was wrong with him? Didn't he understand how scared she was?

She rummaged through her luggage, quickly located the flashlight, flicked it on and shone its beam across the trunks and branches of the nearest trees.

She didn't have too far to look for Toby. He was hung up in a tree not too far from where she was standing. However, he seemed to be unconscious and his feet were dangling about a foot off the ground.

Denise hurried over to his side.

"Hey, baby, are you okay?"

Then she gasped in shock. Toby was far from okay. In fact, from the evidence confronting her, he was quite dead. She needed no medical degree to determine this, as his neck was twice as long as usual.

Amazingly, the brutal swipe of the creature's tail had flung Toby Morales among the trees in such a way that the upper part of his body had become entangled in a clump of low-hanging branches. His head was still wedged between three of those branches, but his neck was clearly broken as evidenced by the grotesque stretching of his neck.

Denise stood there shaking with horror, fighting not to pee herself. Toby's eyes were closed, but there was blood on his lips.

Shit! I need to get away from here right now.

Denise did not dare scream for help. Even though Toby's death was both accidental and incidental, she remembered the crocodile's eyes, those twin gleaming orange lamps. Possibly because of the amount of Agent Orange that it had consumed, the scaly reptile giant had entered the river to cool off; and it had even seemed quite stoned while departing. But herself making a loud noise might both bring the gator to its senses again and also bring it back to her.

So, I need to quietly sneak away from here, she thought with a sad glance at Toby's dangling corpse, which, if the truth was told, resembled a Christmas tree decoration.

Denise's horror was about to increase.

She stood there shivering and indecisive. Confusion filled her from head to toe. She snapped the flashlight off. She'd just realized that it pin-pointed her location for the 'gator' as dangerously as smoking a cigarette in a trench at night during wartime was a great way to get one's head blown apart by an enemy sniper.

But in the end, the decision was made for her. Alerted to nearby movement by the loud rustle of leaves, Denise spun around. Something was nearby, that was for sure. She could hear heavy breathing mere yards away from her.

She quickly flicked her flashlight back on, and shone it through the trees.

Dammit! How could I become so lost in thought?

Then she screamed and almost flung the flashlight away due to sheer fright. The giant gator was standing opposite her, the beam of her flashlight making its eyes seem like vehicle lights. As if blinded by the light, the gator opened its huge jaws and waved its head from side to side while grunting angrily.

Denise stood frozen, unsure in which direction to flee.

Then the huge animal lurched into motion. It came straight at her, its squat scaly body seeming to slide across the grass. Fifteen yards quickly became ten, then five, then . . .

At the very last second before the creature would have snapped her in two, Denise realized she had a way to escape it. She turned and ran to the tree that had caught Toby. Once there, she grabbed hold of a low-hanging branch and began climbing. Thankfully, the tree's branches were close together and made the going easy. On her way up she stepped on Toby's head and almost slipped off of his hair. (This resulted in Toby's slipping down between the branches holding him up, but only to become entangled in another group of branches lower down the tree trunk.)

But luck was with Denise, and very soon she reached a middle branch about ten feet off the ground. From here she stared down at the massively large gator, which was unable to climb up the tree and so began prowling around it in frustration.

Denise felt intense anger radiating from the creature, which likely had no idea what was irritating it so much. She cursed Max for conceiving of Agent Orange, then she cursed her own stupidity for hooking up with a drug pusher boyfriend.

She shone her flashlight beam down at it. The light seemed to agitate it, so she turned the light off again. Now the darkness worried her. All she had for lighting now was the moon, which was reflected off of the river surface.

Denise understood that she was trapped up here in the tree for as long as the gator remained below. It had stopped prowling around now, and was looking up at her, tilting its long head for a better view. Denise began praying, that in addition to making the creature both larger and faster, its Agent Orange consumption hadn't also enabled the damn gator to jump like a basketballer.

Denis was taking great care to maintain her balance on her tree branch.

One slip and I'm gator food.

But she almost lost her balance when a series of noisy impacts rocked the tree. Looking down, she realized that the gator had been biting at something. Switching on her flashlight again revealed what the animal had done. She was just in time to watch the gator gulp down the lower half of Toby's body, clothes, shoes, and all, leaving the upper portion that it couldn't reach dangling from the tree, with half of its innards in turn dangling out of the severed abdomen.

Denise fainted from the sheer gory horror of the sight, the flashlight falling from her fingers and landing on the gator's snout.

It was a sheer miracle that Denise herself didn't fall out of the tree after falling unconscious.

CHAPTER 21

After a while of prowling around the tree, Bill the crocodile waddled back over to the river again.

Bill, unaware that he'd unwittingly drugged himself while consuming the package of raw chicken, felt very restless. No sooner had he submerged himself into the river, than he once more felt like leaving it and prowling through the forest.

The Agent Orange was still at work in the crocodile. The crocodile didn't have much of a brain to begin with, but what little consciousness he did have was now being hardwired for violent behavior by the orange chemical now flowing from his digestive system to his bloodstream.

For Bill, violence was no longer linked to just feeding and establishing mating and territorial rights. Slowly but assuredly, with his change in perspective almost matching pace with the changes to his eyes (which grew larger and brighter by the minute), violence was becoming a way of life for Bill the crocodile.

And already, just like the rats and rabbits in Max's laboratory, Bill had gotten completely addicted to Agent Orange.

CHAPTER 22

After dinner was over in the Bentley household, Gary and Charlotte Bentley sat side-by-side on their living room couch and watched television. Today had been supposed to be Gary's day off, but instead—thanks to the accident they'd encountered on the way home—it had ended up like a working day too.

Gary sighed at the memory. Immediately he'd seen the crash, he'd slipped out of the pleasant recreational frame of mind that meeting their old friends had created and entered back into 'forest ranger mode,' as his wife jokingly referred to it. Doing so had instantly undone all the relaxing benefits of his having a day off of work.

Ah, this is the life, Gary thought now as he poured Charlotte a fresh glass of wine. *Yeah, the sweet and quiet country life. Nothing but trees and animal all around; no noisy people or noisy cars to drive one crazy.*

At the moment, with his loving wife by his side, and a glass of dry wine in hand, Gary Bentley was trying to reclaim the pleasant feeling that he'd enjoyed for the early part of that Saturday. He had an early shift tomorrow and intended to relax a bit tonight.

Part of his relaxation plan involved getting Charlotte into bed. To this end, Gary had made certain he was the one with the TV remote control. The one thing he didn't want happening was Charlotte getting sucked into listening to some miserable news bulletin that might put a damper on the romantic mood that currently existed between them.

He'd found a 1940's romantic comedy that he knew Charlotte was partial to, and which he didn't mind either, and they'd been laughing through the film for an hour. Gary sipped his wine, flung an arm around Charlotte's shoulder and let his fingers delve lower and lower into the top of her dress. Charlotte giggled and snuggled up closer to him.

By this time Gary Bentley had a stiff hard-on that Charlotte was coyly pretending not to notice, and judging from the way she gasped and her breathing sped up when he slipped his hand down into her bra and cupper her right breast, they might not make to the bedroom tonight.

Yes, Gary was feeling really good.

But then a commercial break came on and the first commercial was advertising WhiteMax Toothpaste.

And it was then that Charlotte turned to Gary and said, "Hey, darling, I almost forgot to show you what I found out in the woods today."

With those words Gary had a sudden surreal feeling of trouble lingering on his horizon. For an obscure and unspecific reason, the romantic mood seemed about to break for the second time today.

"What you talking about, honey?" he asked Charlotte who was already slipping out of his grasp.

"Hold on and I show you," she replied, while he tried to stop her by grabbing her ass. But she was already too far away and so he was forced to wait and see what she wanted to show him.

Charlotte was back in less than a minute, pulling something out of her handbag.

"Here's what I found," she said, handing an ivory-colored conical object to him. "It must've have come from a bear or mountain lion. Or possibly from a Great Dane."

Gary accepted the object from her and turned it over and over. It was a tooth, no doubt about that. But it was a strange tooth, one that didn't look like it would fit inside of a bear's mouth. Nor could it be from a bobcat.

"Where'd you find this?" he asked Charlotte, while examining it some more. No, this wasn't a dog's tooth either.

Now that she'd handed him the tooth, Charlotte had discarded her purse on the floor and was making herself comfortable beside Gary again.

"It was on the forest floor, near the overturned van," she replied simply and returned her attention to the television, where the commercials had just ended and the movie was continuing. She picked up her glass of wine from the end table and relaxed against her husband.

Gary once more draped his arm around Charlotte's shoulders. But while she concentrated on the film, which had just reached the point where the heroine was threatened with both rape and death by the villain, Gary found himself unable to watch the film; for the moment, his full attention was taken up by the tooth in his hand. Something about the tooth struck him as extremely familiar. It clearly came from a carnivore; but he couldn't place which one of them; and in his work as a forest ranger he'd encountered lots of hungry animals.

After a vague glance at the TV, he turned the tooth over in his free hand again. Closest he could liken it to was a shark's tooth; it had that kind of triangular symmetry to it. And yet, he didn't think it came from a shark; it was too thick for that, though he couldn't be sure. And anyway, where would one find a shark's tooth in the forest? Though the possibility did exist of some kid flinging one out from a window while the family SUV ferried them back from a seaside vacation. Which was most likely the explanation, as the accident site hadn't been far off from the road, and was well within range of an object cast from a moving vehicle.

Onscreen, the hero had just rescued the heroine, and was kissing her while the villain fled on a horse.

"Hey, why'd you stop?" Charlotte asked Gary.

"Huh?" he asked as her voice drew him back into the present. "Stop what?"

She giggled and then leaned up to kiss him. "Oh, you know, the fingers-in-bra thing you were doing before the commercial came on."

That was all the invitation Gary needed. He dropped the strange tooth on the end table and then grabbed Charlotte in both hands and began peeling her clothes off, while onscreen the hero fought his climactic battle with the movie's villain.

Gary had been right, they never made it into the bedroom; they made love right there on the living room couch, while the film's closing credits providing them with sweet, romantic music.

CHAPTER 23

Dean Wilson and Monique Travers arrived at the Sleepaway Campground at around ten p.m.

When they pulled up into the parking lot, the sickle moon was high in the sky, and for the most part the world seemed asleep.

Dean parked the Chrysler and she and Monique got out and looked around. The wind blowing through the parking lot played havoc with Monique's hair. Dean, who was rather butch and sported a blonde crew-cut, was amused by Monique's futile attempts to control her long brown hair.

"Baby, you should have done that while we were in the car," Dean said. She stepped close to Monique. "Here, let me give you a hand with it."

Monique surrendered her hair to Dean, who quickly collected it together and clipped it in place.

"There," she said, leaning in to kiss Monique on the lips. The pair had been lovers for two weeks now and the novelty of their relationship (for Monique at least) meant that each time they got intimate in public, the previously straight Monique kept looking over her shoulder to see who was watching.

"Relax, no one's watching," Dean said, reading the expression on her girlfriend's face despite the darkness.

The girls kissed and hugged in the deserted parking lot, and when they separated, Monique asked: "Any word yet from Toby?"

Dean shook her head and looked pissed off. "None. I hope he doesn't intend to stand me up. I don't wanna have to drive back into Elkins to buy the chicken for tomorrow's barbeque."

"I still don't see why we couldn't buy the meat ourselves. We passed enough supermarkets on our drive here."

Dean scowled in the darkness. "I already explained that; Toby offered to buy the meat for me. He wants to sell drugs to the guys at our party tomorrow. Should be at least twenty people coming over here to the camp—lots of new clients for Toby."

"Oh yeah," Monique said with downturned lips. She disliked Toby, whom she found creepy. "You were saying he's got this new drug he keeps raving about."

Dean had moved to the trunk of their vehicle and was unloading their camping things. "Oh yeah, about that new orange crack of his that he's selling," she told Monique while handing her the inflatable tent, "don't you dare touch that stuff. As far as I can tell from the news, it'll drive you crazy."

Monique nodded. She had no intention of using crack cocaine anyway. She was a well-brought up girl, one who'd been schooled in the doctrine that drug use fucked you up. Monique believed that. She worked as a nurse and so got to see lots of drug cases; both the users and those they hurt when their addiction got the better of them, which happened regularly. Oh no, neither active nor passive involvement in the drug scene was her thing; there was no way that she wanted any of that happening to her.

Dean taught high school mathematics and seemed more comfortable around drug use, but Monique had no interest in narcotics.

All Monique desired this weekend was some quality time with her girlfriend and lots of sweet sex.

"Alright, we're good," Dean said, shutting the trunk. "We'll come back for the grill and other shit in the morning." She slipped on a knapsack and waited for Monique to do the same.

Then, carrying the inflatable mattress between them, the girlfriends set off along the western campground trail. Monique carried a bag of food in her free hand, while Dean shone a torchlight on the trail to illuminate their way.

"I've been up here before," Monique said as they walked between the trees to the accompanying sounds of night critters. "Why aren't we camping down by the river near the parking lot?"

"Too many people over there," Dean said. "The way we're headed, we'll still be pitching our tent near the river, but we'll have more privacy." She leaned over and kissed Monique. "If you understand what I mean."

Monique did. She felt the delicious anticipatory thrill of a thousand tingles running up and down her body.

Dean got out her cellphone again and once more tried to get Toby on the line. "Keeps hitting voicemail," she said in disgust after two attempts.

"Maybe his battery ran down. He might be waiting for us, like you said."

"Doubt it. His car's not in the lot back there."

Monique mused on that. "Don't you have his girlfriend's number? What's her name again?"

"Denise?" Dean shook her head. "No, I don't." Then she added, "Still, it's possible that you're right and they're both already there waiting for us."

They reached the fork in the trail and turned left towards the river. After walking about a hundred yards towards the river, Dean's flashlight picked out several pieces of scattered luggage lying on the ground.

"Hey, what's going on here?" she said.

Monique also saw what she had. "Looks like there's been some kind of a fight over there."

Dean played the flashlight beam over the grass. "Doesn't seem to be anyone around," she concluded. "But what the hell happened?"

"I'm not liking the looks of this," Monique said. "All of a sudden I really wish we'd brought your brother's gun along with us. Sure, I'm all for experiencing the 'wonderful wild,' but so are all the serial killers too."

"Calm down," Dean told her. "Let's have a look and—"

"Hey, someone's coming!" Monique yelped.

Dean looked and saw that, yes, someone was running out from the midst of the trees. Her first instinct was to grab hold of Monique and run for their lives, but then she saw that the approaching person was a young woman, and was someone she knew.

"Isn't that Toby's girlfriend Denise?" Monique asked as they both dropped their ends of the inflatable tent and stared. "What the hell's the matter with her?"

"She looks fucking terrified," Dawn said, now wishing she'd agreed to Monique's request that she borrow her elder brother's gun for the weekend.

Denise had now reached them. "Listen, there's no time to talk, we've gotta get the hell away from here!" she told them, sounding like she was screaming with the volume turned down.

Dean tried to calm the panicked young woman down. "What's the matter? What happened here? And where the hell is Toby?"

Denise's response was to attempt to run past them, but they held her tight so she couldn't get away. Monique looked at Dean, who nodded back at her. Whatever was going on here, they both wanted to get to the root of it.

"Where's Toby?" Dean asked again, in a more authoritative tone of voice, the one she used with her high school students when they were getting out of hand. "What the hell happened over there?"

"Toby's dead!" Denise shrieked at both of them and once again tried to free herself and run away from them. "A giant gator broke his neck and then ate his legs!"

Her explanation seemed ludicrous to Dean and Monique. The fear that had been building in both young women was almost immediately defused by amusement.

"Honey, there's no gators in West Virginia," Monique said.

"None at all, except in the zoos," Dean said. Still keeping a tight hold on Denise, she nodded at her girlfriend. "Come on, let's go see what really happened. I'm not ruling out the fact that Toby's dead. But if he is, he most likely overdosed on that new drug of his." She shone her flashlight beam in Denise's face, causing her to blink. "She's high on drugs too. I see shit like this all the time with my students; someone experiments with LSD and starts thinking he's living in *The Mandalorian.*"

"I just hope she hasn't killed Toby herself, 'cos we can clearly see that a fight happened over there," Monique agreed.

CHAPTER 24

"Fucking let go of me, you two lezzie idiots!" Denise screamed at Dean and Monique as they dragged her back towards her scattered luggage. "There's a killer gator in the river and it's gonna eat all of us!"

But clearly neither woman believed her. In the darkness, she couldn't make out their faces as they forced her back with them, but the tightness of their grip on her was evidence enough that they believed she was guilty of something.

I'm gonna die tonight, Denise thought glumly, her gaze focused on the moon, which tonight seemed to be the only sane and unchanging thing in her situation, a situation which grew crazier by the second. *There's a giant gator with headlamp eyes in the nearby river and these two idiots are pulling me back to it!*

After that thought, she more or less went limp between Dean and Monique and let them drag her passively along with them.

"No sign of blood here," Monique said, when they reached the scattered luggage. "But there is sort of a weird smell, like someone dumped garbage in the river."

Dean had meanwhile noticed the two gator-smashed cellphones. "Why'd you break the phones?" she asked Denise in a menacing voice. "You didn't want someone to dial 9-1-1?"

Denise felt relieved that Dean wasn't asking for her chicken for tomorrow's barbecue. If Dean mentioned the chicken, Denise would attempt to kill her and that would be that.

"Girl, where's Toby?" Monique asked in a suspicious voice.

"Come with me and I'll show you two lezzie idiots," Denise said. "You're gonna get us all killed."

"Shut up and take us there," Dean said. "Try to escape again and I'm gonna hurt you."

"Call us lezzie idiots one more time and I'll hurt you even worse," Monique added.

Denise didn't argue. Feeling her life ticking away by the second, she walked her two lesbian captors over to the tree where Toby's remains hung.

Once beside the tree in question, Dean and Monique instantly let Denise go.

"The fuck happened here?" Dean said in a horrified voice.

Now there was no question of doubting Denise's innocence. Even the craziest serial killer couldn't have fucked Toby up like this.

"Where the fuck is the rest of him?" Monique asked in a horrified voice as Dean's flashlight revealed the gory spectacle of the upper half of Toby Morales dangling by a neck that was now at least three times as long as normal. If Toby had been a church bell, his dangling intestines would be the bell rope to ring him by.

Dean bent over and threw up. Monique slumped against Dean. Denise at first thought she was gripping Dean for comfort from the horrible vision facing them, but no, Monique had fainted. She dropped to the forest floor the way Toby's innards dropped out of him when the gator chomped him in two.

And then suddenly, Denise heard the leaves rustling ominously. The gator was nearby.

Denise turned around. She did so slowly, as if seeking not to attract attention to herself. Yeah, she'd been right. The gator was watching them. Its orange eyes almost made the forest brighter.

Without further ado, Denise leapt up and once again began climbing up into the tree.

When she was halfway to her safe branch, she looked back down. Dean was shining her flashlight up at her.

"What the hell are you doing? What's up there?"

"Safety," Denise replied, then she waved down at Dean. "Goodbye, girl."

"What the fuck are you talking about?"

"Look behind you." With that advice given, Denise resumed her climb to safety.

She didn't look down even when she heard Dean screaming in fear. Not until she was safely back on her branch, did she turn to watch was what happening below.

Monique was still out cold on the forest floor.

Meanwhile, the giant gator had Dean clamped between its jaws. The beast had her around the middle; Dean's head and shoulders projected out of the animal's mouth on one side and her legs showed on the other side. Dean was screaming for help. She still had the flashlight and waved it wildly as the gator shook her left and right, the flashlight beam splattering the leaves of the surrounding trees with splashes of green.

And then, uncharacteristically for a member of its species on land, the animal went into a gator roll, its scary eyes seeming to blink in and out of existence as its horizontal position altered in relation to the ground.

Somewhere in the middle of this rolling motion, Dean's spine audibly broke and both of her legs bloodily separated from her torso. Also, during this 'rolling' period was when Monique roused from her faint, and on seeing what was happening to her girlfriend, she instantly fainted again.

The gator stopped rolling over the forest floor, and once it was properly balanced again on its short legs, it swallowed what remained of Dean. Then it walked over to Monique and without waiting for her to wake up from her second faint, it bit her head off and swallowed that too.

Denise watched all of this from the safety of her branch. By now she was traumatized. The violence bounced off of her soul like a ball.

After eating Monique's head, the gator lay down beneath the tree and seemed to fall asleep. It spread its blood-splattered bulk over Monique's decapitated corpse as if protecting its food supply from thieves.

However, Denise was far from deceived. She was certain the gator wasn't really asleep.

For sure, the nightmare creature was simply playing opossum; it might have shut its large orange eyes, but that was no guarantee of her safety if she attempted to climb down, which would actually be impossible now without her stepping down onto the creature's back, which was as out of the question as her jumping the ten feet from her branch of safety to the ground, the noise of which landing would be guaranteed to rouse the gator from its faked slumber.

So, with the part of her mind that wasn't yet scared shitless, Denise Higgins determined to remain up there in the tree until someone arrived to help her.

Help had to arrive at some point. Denise knew it had to. This nightmare she was currently living had to end sooner or later.

CHAPTER 25

It was 2 a.m. when Gary Bentley woke up to use the bathroom.

After relieving himself, Gary went back to lie beside Charlotte, but now discovered he couldn't get back to sleep.

He lay tossing and turning beside Charlotte in their bed until he realized that his restlessness would wake her up too. So, after kissing his slumbering wife gently on her cheek, Gary got out of bed again, wrapped a dressing gown around himself and went to make himself a drink.

It was while he was sitting in the dark with a whiskey in his hand, watching the television with the sound off, that he remembered the strange tooth Charlotte had found.

He leaned over and picked up the tooth from the end table where he'd earlier dropped it. Once more he began studying the tooth, trying to figure out what sort of animal it had come from. Once more he had little luck.

The thickness of the base of the tooth seemed to indicate that it wouldn't fit closely to other teeth in its owner's mouth; that was the problem. Now, what kind of animal had a mouth full of sparse teeth?

And then finally, on a hunch, Gary telephoned his son Mike, who was studying marine biology at Pennsylvania State University at their Center for Marine Science and Technology.

It was early in the morning and Mike would most likely be asleep, but if he wasn't Gary wanted his input on his problem.

Thankfully, Mike Bentley wasn't asleep. "Hi, dad. What's up with you calling me so late at night?"

Gary laid out the problem for Mike.

"Take three or four pictures of the tooth from different angles and send them to me," Mike said.

Gary did so, and there was communication silence for about three minutes. Gary sipped his whiskey and put the phone on speaker, a strange expectancy settling over him as the break in communication lengthened.

Finally, Mike's voice came over the line again. Gary picked up the cellphone. "Yeah, kid, what you find out?"

"No, dad, it's not a shark tooth. It's from an alligator."

Gary felt like someone had kicked him in the chest. "An alligator?"

"Yep," Mike replied. "Either a gator or a croc, in any case the tooth is from a crocodilian." There was a pause when Gary heard the kid shifting papers. "I'm guessing 'gator,' though since crocs aren't routinely found over here."

"Crocodilian," Gary said silently to himself as he digested this info.

"One other thing," Mike added, when his father didn't comment.

"Yeah? What's that, son?"

"From the looks of things, that tooth you've got there has only just been recently knocked out. The freshness of the break is obvious."

Gary put down his whiskey and turned the tooth over and studied the cracked-off end. "Mike, I'm curious; what would it take to knock the tooth out?"

"Well, this seems to be one of its rear teeth, so it'd have to quite strong impact. Something like a fall, or if it slammed into something, or a rock hit it in the mouth, or if the tooth snagged on something really hard."

"How about a car accident?" Gary asked. "Would that do it?"

"A car accident?" Mike laughed. "Nah, dad, I think the airbags would protect the gator from harm, so long as it had its seatbelt on."

Father and son both laughed at that.

After Mike had hung up, Gary picked up his whiskey again.

Okay, now let me think this through, he thought. *Charlotte said she found this tooth close to that crashed van yesterday evening. We also heard on the news that a crocodile had been abducted from an Ohio animal facility. And then, there's two more facts to consider. Firstly, that the back of that van was busted open by the crash, and also, what my wife pointed out to me as we drove back home, that those two brothers were acting really suspicious, like they didn't want any other accounts of the accident coming to light.*

His eyes cloudy with concern, Gary Bentley finished off his whiskey and then sat back thinking.

There was something else bothering him, something strange that he'd noticed at the crash site, but which for the moment had slipped his mind. After he'd put a little effort into remembering the sequence of events that had succeeded, he and Charlotte's noticing the crashed car, it suddenly came back to him:

Oh, yes, I was wondering at the time why the side of the van seemed deformed, almost as if . . . he frowned as the implications solidified in his mind . . . *as if something large and angry, like a bear, for instance, had been slamming its body against it . . . from the inside.*

Gary sighed. *If that stolen crocodile is loose in the woods now, we've got a huge problem,* he thought. *Because . . . that crash occurred right next to the Sleepaway Campground.*

Now he felt both alarmed and frustrated. It was too late at night for him to begin making emergency calls to the ranger station, and yet it was also too early in the morning for him to set out for the Sleepaway Campground.

And besides, I gotta make sure first that the missing crocodile is here in WV before I alarm everyone on a flimsy suspicion.

Gary couldn't wait for morning to come.

CHAPTER 26

Over at the Teter Creek Lake trailer park, and at about the same time that Gary Bentley was climbing back into bed to catch some sleep before the morning's search for the missing crocodile, Jessie Barnes got out of she and Max's bed and wandered into their living room.

Jessie needed to get high and Max stored all the Agent Orange in the living room. Max hid the drugs he synthesized in the back of the armchair nearest to the television. As his girlfriend, Jessie had free access to anything she wanted, and could take as much as she liked, so long as she only opened the armchair hiding compartment when there were no witnesses.

Jessie got out five rocks from the armchair compartment and shut it up again. She smirked as the lock clicked shut on the drugs. Unknown to Max's dealers Toby and Denise, Max had been making Agent Orange at a breakneck rate and stockpiling it here against his grand takeover of the entire American northeast.

Jessie didn't care. She wasn't an ambitious woman and was primarily with Max for the rock anyway. Even though she often cautioned Max to be careful with how he conducted his business, her motivation for doing this was self-interest; if Max got busted and went to jail, or worse, got killed by rival dealers, she'd have no more source of Agent Orange.

And Agent Orange was the ultimate high. No arguments there, even though the drug tended to make Jessie as mad as hell with her chemist boyfriend. Even though he was well acquainted with her murderous impulses when in 'crackhead mode' Max really had no idea how close Jessie had come to killing him on several occasions.

She packed her crackpipe with Agent Orange and lit up. Oh, the sweet bliss she felt as the opaque fumes spiraled into her mouth. It was a transcendent feeling.

Jessie got up and walked into Max's laboratory. Suddenly she felt wicked and felt like teasing Max's little lab animals.

The moment she shut the lab door behind her, the animals all came alive. The lab was in darkness, so Jessie flicked the lights on, but even before she did so, she could hear the little beasts flinging themselves against the walls of their cages in her direction.

At first, she found it amusing to watch them fight against the steel, trying to reach her, their little orange eyes gleaming with an anger their little brains found impossible to comprehend. Their teeth gnashing against their cages until their mouths bled.

But her pleasure quickly waned. Tonight, the orange-eyed rats, rabbits, and other rodents looked so intent on attacking her if they only could, that for once Jessie lost her interest in rubbing their helplessness in their little faces. She suddenly had a picture of what they could and would do to her if, heaven forbid, some unforeseen accident let them out of their cages.

Suddenly feeling magnanimous, Jessie decided to give the caged animals a special treat. She hurried back into the living room and opened up Max's hiding place again. From it she took a whole package of Agent Orange and then returned to the lab, where she dropped one or two of the little orange 'marshmallows' through the roof of each cage.

The animals all attacked the drug in frenzies, wolfing it down in violent abandon. While they ate it, Jessie lit up her crack pipe and got high as well.

But it surprised Jessie Barnes that, even after she'd fed them all like this, even after she'd been so nice to them tonight, sharing her drugs with them, Max's little zoo of caged rodents regarded her with even greater anger than before. In fact, they seemed to hate her now. They seemed jealous that she had such easy access to this pleasure that was denied them.

Once all the Agent Orange was gone, the test animals resumed throwing themselves against the walls of their cages, trying to reach Jessie again.

Fuck you all, you ungrateful little shits! she finally decided in anger. *Oh, this is the first and the last time you'll ever get any drugs from me.*

Carrying the rest of the stuff in the bag, she left the laboratory and went to smoke her crack in the living room, where she didn't have to look at the nasty little creatures.

CHAPTER 27

His belly full of human flesh, Bill the crocodile dozed contentedly beneath the large oak tree in which Denise Higgins was trapped. The animal dreamt his animal dreams and the night hours passed swiftly, with Bill not even waking up when, with no options, Denise raised her skirt and peed out of the tree on top of him. The urine was simply another of the smells of the summer night that wafted into the slumbering reptile's nostrils and out again. If anything, the subconscious impression that a fourth human meal was close by helped the animal sleep better.

However, all was not well in Bill's life. Slowly but surely, the drug he'd accidentally consumed began eating away at him, creeping into his dreams and agitating them, turning pleasant slumber into a restless sequence of images that had the crocodile shaking his bulk left and right until the force of his impact against the tree almost toppled Denise down on top of him.

Dawn was breaking when Bill awoke. And now the crocodile had a serious craving for . . . something. Bill was surrounded by corpses, and could also both smell and see the quaking human female on the tree branch above him, but for the moment none of those interested him. Instead, his extremely sensitive nostrils fastened on a smell, a strangely familiar smell that, if crocodiles were a more intelligent species, Bill might have realized was the same smell that had been mixed in with the chicken he had consumed yesterday.

Bill had a sudden craving for more Agent Orange.

With an addict's strong resolution, the crocodile abandoned the base of the tree and headed for the river, stomping Dean Wilson's remains into the grass as he went.

The smell was distant, coming from downriver, from a place where there also seemed to be more humans who might provide him with a satisfying breakfast.

Bill had no idea he was smelling Max's laboratory, where the drug called Agent Orange was synthesized. He had no idea he was a drug addict now chasing his next fix. All he knew what that he had to follow that fascinating smell, borderline unpleasant though it was, to its source.

His junkie craving, a strange and unfamiliar appetite he was just becoming aware of, demanded that he find and consume as much of the pungent substance as he possibly could.

And so, following his nose, Bill slipped into the river and began swimming down to Teter Creek Lake. He was in no hurry. As he swam, the summoning smell grew stronger, as did another even more familiar smell, the smell of raw meat.

By the time Bill reached Teter Creek Lake, the smell of succulent dead flesh was so thick in the water that he decided to detour from his initial destination and head for it instead.

Also attracting him in that direction was a familiar human smell— that of the two humans who'd disturbed yesterday's lunch.

Lacking any understanding of the fact that he had been abducted or of the reasons thereof, the crocodile simply viewed the two Pollak brothers as competition that he needed to eliminate if he was to establish his territorial feeding rights to these parts. The competitors would either need to be killed or scared away, so they ceased to compete with him for food like they had done yesterday.

The Agent Orange smell was nearby now, so close that its presence had the aura of an answered prayer to the crocodile.

CHAPTER 28

Once his alarm clock went off, Gary Bentley leapt out of bed and ran into the bathroom to freshen up. He was a man on a mission, and yet it still took him longer than he'd intended to get ready for work.

It was Sunday morning; Charlotte was still fast asleep. She turned over once and smiled up at him. "What's the rush, honey?"

He waved her back to sleep and continued putting his uniform on.

By the time he ran out the front door of his house, alarm bells were ringing in his mind like it was judgment day.

He was moving so fast that he almost tramped on some of Charlotte's domesticated raccoons, which were waiting on the front porch for Charlotte to wake up and serve them breakfast.

After avoiding the raccoons, Gary felt his routine irritation toward his wife for insisting on feeding the local wildlife and thus breaking up their usual nocturnal foraging habits. But his anger didn't have sufficient fuel to linger long. He was too preoccupied with thoughts of the danger that might be lurking in the nearby woods, to grumble about the harmless animals on his front porch.

Gary leapt into his forest ranger pickup truck, then leapt down again and ran back into the house to grab his shotgun. He grabbed a box of spare shells too.

Driving away from his house, Gary Bentley couldn't avoid feeling panicked. He'd done some online research on the missing Ohio crocodile and had become scared on realizing how large it was.

Sixteen feet long? What the hell were those thieves thinking? Where the hell did they plan to hide the damn croc? Where were they gonna ship it too? Back to fucking Africa?

Now, as he steered the ranger pickup truck onto the US Route 33 highway, he forced himself to calm down

It's best I don't get ahead of myself now and start a panic over nothing at all. The missing croc may be in the woods near the campground or it may not be. There's still the chance that Mike was wrong about the tooth coming from a crocodilian at all; even if it is, there's likely a logical explanation to all this.

But he knew he was deceiving himself. His son Mike was a straight-A college student and was never wrong about shit like that.

So, the croc is out there in our WV woods and the most logical place it's gonna head for is the Shaver's Fork River, or maybe Teter Creek, which connects to Teter Creek Lake, where we've got that trailer park with all the senior citizens. This is shaping up to be a major disaster, and what's driving me nuts is that I've gotta make certain my suspicions are right before I alert anyone. Alright, river or lake, which of 'em? Which do I search first? I'll head for the campground, since that's nearer to where the crash occurred. Then to Teter Creek Lake.

***

Even though nothing seemed amiss when Gary pulled up in the Sleepaway Campground parking lot, he didn't feel any less worried. He quickly got out of the pickup truck and looked around at the nearest trees for signs of animal trouble. He saw nothing amiss, and the trail leading to the river was deserted too. No corpses littered the bridge and from this distance he saw no severed body parts such as a ravaging gator might leave.

Finally, Gary headed off down the westward trail with his shotgun in hand and his pockets bulging with spare ammo.

Choosing the western forest trail had been an entirely instinctive decision. On his regular patrols of this campground, Gary always walked in a circle that went in this direction, walking the western trail to the farther bridge over the river, and then crossing that bridge and walking the opposite river bank back to the nearer bridge that he was now leaving behind. It was an effective patrol circuit that easily enabled him to check on both the cabins across the river and the campers scattered in the forest.

Gary saw no signs of trouble until he arrived at the fork in the trail where one had a choice of either continuing west into further woodland, or of turning north to join the river. A short distance after turning north, he came upon an inflatable mattress that had seemingly been abandoned in the middle of the trail.

If that was odd, odder still were the bags scattered around a short distance ahead of there. Gary hurried over to the bags. There were two of these with their contents strewn across the grass. Male and female clothes and shoes; cosmetics; snacks of various kinds; and also what looked like a party bag of pills and marijuana joints. Another oddity were the two smashed cellphones that lay one on top of the other, their screens shattered.

Okay, this looks bad, Gary thought, gripping the shotgun tight. *This looks real bad. At the very least someone and their girlfriend had a bad fight here, possibly over drugs. Shit.*

His concerns only increased when he noticed several impressions on the forest floor that might or might not have been animal footprints. He was well in sight of the river now and wanted to rush down there and check for more footprints, which would be sufficient evidence to get wildlife services down here fast, but the scattered human belongings on the grass made him pause.

Where's the people that own all this stuff? There's gotta be at least two of 'em.

"Hey, is there anyone here!?" He shouted. "Hey, I'm a forest ranger. Where are you guys!? Are you all okay?"

Gary waited for a reply, and then yelled out again: "Hey, anyone around here? Your stuff's scattered everywhere! What happened!? Where is everyone!?"

"Yes, yes, I'm here!" a female voice yelled back over on his left. "Please come over here! It's gone now!"

It's gone now?

With the shotgun held poised to shoot, Gary ran over toward the female voice.

"Here, here, I'm up in a tree!"

Gary stopped and felt sick. Only once before in his life had he seen this sort of physical carnage. He was staring at three corpses; one male and two female, and for the life of him, he couldn't tell which corpse was in the worst condition. One of the female corpses was headless, and lay at the foot of the tree from which the male corpse dangled by a neck that was now four or five times its original length. The dead young man's head was trapped between two branches about four feet off of the ground, and all of his lower body from the navel down was missing. However, the horrible elongation of his neck meant that his truncated torso was dangling mere inches above the forest floor.

The other young woman lay in two separate parts over on Gary's left. Her head and shoulders lay at the base of one tree and her legs lay at the base of another tree five or six yards away. Her entire midriff—breasts to hips—was missing.

Gary also noted that the grass here was flattened, as if something huge had rolled back and forth over it. The grass was also brightly splattered with lots of blood, but, considering the gruesome events that must have occurred here, Gary figured that was only to be expected.

The young woman who'd summoned Gary was now descending the tree from which the young man was dangling. At a point near the ground, she used the dead boy's shoulders as her ladder, which stretched his neck even more and resulted in his torso finally touching the ground.

Once her own feet touched the ground, the young woman ran across to Gary and held him tight. "Oh, thank God that you finally came!" she wept on him, her tears of relief quickly wetting Gary's shirt. "Thank God you came! I've been trapped up in that tree all night long while it slept!"

Gary hugged the distraught young woman. "While what slept?" he asked gently. The question was merely to confirm what he already suspected.

The question made her leap back and start at him. "It was a gator!" she shrieked, waving her arms wildly like she was losing her mind right here and right now. "The biggest gator I ever saw in my life!"

"It was actually a crocodile," Gary said, and then felt foolish for pointing that out.

But his young companion clearly hadn't heard him. She jabbed her fingers around at the three dead young people and kept talking. "The gator came out of nowhere and it . . . it killed everyone; killed my friends. The gator . . . it had these huge orange eyes and—"

"Back up a bit," Gary told the girl. "What did you just say about the crocodile having huge orange eyes?"

She nodded fiercely. "It did, it did. See, what happened was that my boyfriend had this new drug he was selling called Agent Orange, and we hid it in a bag of raw chicken for a barbeque! But the gator smelt the chicken and followed us here and then ate the whole bag and that was when its eyes changed color and . . ."

Listening to the half-crazed young woman explain what had happened made Gary Bentley feel sick.

Oh, fuck, not a-damn-gain! he cussed inwardly. *This is gonna be even worse than last time with Elvis the raccoon!*

The girl (who'd now explained that her name was Denise Higgins) finished up her explanation of how she and her drug-dealing boyfriend had accidentally gotten an already huge and dangerous animal jacked up on possibly the one chemical substance on Earth that could make it three or four times as dangerous. According to Denise, the crocodile had eaten five pounds weight of Agent Orange.

That's a whole lot of narcotics for one animal to eat, Gary thought. *It must be a damn junkie by now.* Thoughts that were quickly confirmed by Denise's next words.

"That gator—did you call it a crocodile, mister?—that crocodile acted like it was mad," the girl said. "Yeah, it was raging like a junkie, you know, what they lose their damn minds and don't know what they're doing any more?"

Gary nodded. "Denise, when you called me over, you said it had left. Which way did it go?"

She turned and pointed west. "It went that way. It walked to the river and swam off that way. Yes, that's the way it went. I watched it till it slipped out of sight around the bend in the river."

Gary sighed. *Oh God, no! The damn croc is on its way to Teter Creek Lake!*

Feeling like this was setting up to be the longest day of his life, he unclipped his ranger radio and called Jamie Maloney at the ranger station.

"Hey, Maloney, we've got a problem. A fucking big problem."

"What problem?"

Gary explained. "Listen, you get the Sheriff and all available deputies out here. I'm heading over to Teter Creek Lake to see what I can do. Send the fish department over to the lake to back me up."

CHAPTER 29

This Sunday morning the surface of Teter Creek Lake was calm. There was a slight breeze blowing but nothing sufficient to ripple the water.

Unaware of the problems they'd helped cause, Walt and Jake Pollak sat fishing on the lake in a rented boat. They had two fishing lines, a can of worm bait and to the casual observer appeared to be lazily wasting Sunday morning away.

This was the impression the brothers wished to create and in fact was far from the truth. What the Pollak brothers were really doing here on Teter Creek Lake was fishing for Bill the crocodile.

Of course, one didn't actually *fish* for a crocodile and Jake and Walt's fishing lines looked too weak to even reel in a good-sized bass, but there was literally more to this than met the eye.

Secured to their boat's starboard railing was a steel chain strong enough to bind an elephant. At the end of this unbreakable chain, a skinned dead goat dangled on an equally unbreakable hook. They had chosen a goat over other animals like a piglet or a lamb because that was what Bill had been eating when they'd first encountered him in the animal clinic.

The goat hung in the water with just its ears visible, just sufficient of its body to attract the crocodile. To help Bill better locate them, the Pollak brothers had both skilled the dead goat inside of their boat, and then draped its removed hide over the vessel's edge and the chain.

As Jake had quipped then: "For sure, now there's no way our missing crocodile can miss finding us. This blood and flesh will draw him here for sure."

Before being dropped over the side of the boat, Walt Pollak had injected the skinned goat carcass with a good dose of Xylazine, a fast-acting animal sedative that could be absorbed both through a beast's gums and also the lining of its digestive system.

The brothers had a fresh van parked twenty feet in from the highway, near the point where Teter Creek, a small stream, emptied into Teter Creek Lake. That point had been chosen because the slope of the river bank there was a gradual one, easy to wade through and drag a crocodile along.

Their plan was a simple one; that Bill would smell the goat dangling beneath their boat and attempt to feed on it. Walt and Jake weren't bothered about the distance from their current location to the point where they'd lost the African crocodile; they both knew how good a crocodilian's sense of smell was. Bill was certain to arrive here in the lake sooner than later.

And so, Bill would eat the goat, which meant also eating the hook stuck halfway into it. Once the hook was stuck in the crocodile, he would have little choice but to come along with them when they dragged him back towards the river exit, because hopefully, by then the drug would have kicked in and rendered Bill both sluggish and sleepy. Not unconscious of course; Bill was too big for their little boat to carry as dead weight, but Walt had carefully measured the amount of sedative to what should make Bill docile enough for them to drag him along with them. Both the pain of the hook in his throat and the drug in his system (not to mention the force of the boat's engines) would ensure that the crocodile wouldn't sink but would continue swimming, but only in the direction they wanted him to.

To help this aspect of their plan, the brothers' chosen part of the lake for today's 'fishing' was situated very close to the river exit, as this meant less distance to maneuver their reptile captive once they'd trapped him.

Once in the river, they would drag Bill to the riverbank, dope him properly to sleep and secure his limb with iron chains, then they would winch him out of the water, and load him into their new van.

And then it was farewell campground and welcome paycheck!

Bill hadn't shown up yet, but the day had just dawned and the Pollak brothers had all the time in the world.

***

"Ain't it time yet for you to inject a li'l more sedative in the goat?" Jake asked Walt as they both pretended to fish, though Jake was actually watching YouTube vids on his cellphone.

Walt, who was himself really checking out the local news, checked the time on the screen of his cellphone and then shook his head. "Not yet, bro. That stuff won't really dissolve in the water, but it might wash away if the goat is left hanging too long. Let's it give another hour or so."

That explained, Walt groaned and made himself comfortable in the deck chair. The aches and pains from yesterday's crash were catching up with him now; his hip ached badly, as did both of his arms from straining to keep the van balanced while it was slewing left and right across the road.

His younger brother seemed worse. Jeff had several strips of bandages plastered on his face, and had been walking with a limp since yesterday.

Walt figured that when they collected their paycheck for stealing the crocodile it would be money well earned.

The brothers 'fished' as the daylight established itself across the lake and nearby trailer park. A few other fishermen sailed their craft out on the river. But all headed over towards the far side of the lake, not towards Walt or Jake's boat. Walt was relieved at this; last thing he and his brother needed now was some guy sticking his nose in while they were tugging a stolen and stoned crocodile behind them.

***

All of a sudden, they felt it. Their boat shuddered slightly.

"He's taken the bait," Walt told Jake with satisfaction. The boat shuddered again and from the way the boat dipped significantly it was obvious they'd hooked Bill on the end of their line.

"Okay, now we gotta wait till the hook is properly stuck in his throat," Walt told Jake as they felt additional tugs pulling the boat lower in the water. "That drug works pretty quickly, so we don't need to worry about him fighting us."

Jake nodded and relaxed in his chair, stretching his arms sideways. He had complete faith in his brother's knowledge about things like this.

Walt activated the clock timer on his phone and began a countdown. "Okay, big boy, you're beginning to feel sleepy now. The goat is tasty, sure, but you really wanna just close your eyes and let Uncle Walt and Uncle Jake deliver you to rich Uncle Johnson so they can—"

And just like that, the strain on the boat was suddenly gone. The release of tension occurred so fast that the boat abruptly bobbed up and threw both brothers off of their chairs and down on their backs.

"I think he got away," Jake said from his position on the deck.

"Shit!" Not heeding his aches and pains, Walt leapt to his feet and rushed over to the starboard side of the boat and began hauling in the chain on which they'd suspended the goat. The chain was heavy and Walt soon grunted at Jake to come give him a hand.

Working together, the Pollak brothers pulled the chain up out of the water.

The goat's skinless head hung on the hook, with the rest of its skinless body missing. The hook had been threaded in through its mouth and secured by forcing it out of a hole beneath its ribcage, so how Bill had avoided getting the hook stuck in his throat while swallowing the goat was beyond Walt's understanding. The croc likely had a large tear in his mouth now.

"Shit!" Walt said. "Okay, we've still got a chance to capture him. Bill is sure to be dopy now, unable to resist us. One of us needs to get in the water and look for him. Then—"

"No need to look for him, bro," jake said nervously from the prow of the boat. "He's right here."

Walt at first didn't get what Jake was referring to. But then he saw that Bill was swimming around their boat. Walt watched the crocodile swim around the boat twice, its scales glimmering just below the water surface. He was puzzled. Bill didn't seem tranquilized; he wasn't acting as if the sedative in the goat had affected him in the least. If anything, Bill seemed to be moving faster than was usual for a reptile of his size and species category. Much faster.

And when the crocodile swam round to his side of the boat for a third time, Walt also noticed both that Bill now seemed bigger in size than when they'd stolen him and that his eyes looked like giant oranges.

"Something's wrong," he told Jake.

"We need . . ." Jake began saying.

Walt smiled. He'd seen the *Jaws* movies too. "We need a *bigger* boat? Is that what you were gonna say?"

Jake shook his head. "We need . . ."

Walt laughed. "A *bigger* hook? *Bigger* guns?"

Jake shook his head. "We-we-we n-n-need . . . !"

Walt gave up. "We need *what?*"

"No, no, no! We need to get the fuck outa here!" Jake yelled at him. Then he gestured wildly down into the water, where Bill was just making another round of their boat. "I don't know what the hell is wrong with that goddamn animal, but something is. I ain't never before seen a crocodile or gator acting the way he's doing now, circling this boat like a burglar casing a joint, trying to find his way in. And look at his goddamn eyes. I'm telling you, Walt, something's wrong with this crocodile!"

His worry communicated itself to Walt, who immediately began looking worried. "Shit, man, we can't leave Bill here. We've got to think about our money."

"Screw the money. We can't spend it from a watery grave!"

Jake ran to start up the boat's motor, but that was when the crocodile attacked, coming up from beneath the boat and striking its underside with horrifying impact. The force of impact launched both Walt and Jake over the boat's side and into the water.

Both men were good swimmers, but that was scant consolation when a few seconds later, the two of them realized that they'd been intentionally flung into the water by a ravenous crocodile.

"Quick, back into the boat!" Walt sputtered to his brother a few seconds after both their heads broke the surface of the water.

He and Jake started to swim towards the boat, which was drifting away from them, but was still within easy reach.

I don't see him anywhere around here, Walt thought, as he swam along behind his brother. *That's good. Maybe the dumb animal knocked himself out when he hit the underside of our boat. Yeah, Jake's right; I've had enough of this insane caper. There's lots of easier creatures to ste—*

And that was when Jake gave a loud scream and vanished from sight. There was no resistance, no struggle; Jake vanished as completely as if he'd been sucked down into a black hole.

As for Walt, he'd felt something gigantic brush past him, something that felt as solid as the boat he'd been heading for.

Shocked by the suddenness of what had happened, Walt paused, treading water to overcome his fear and confusion. Walt had twenty feet or so to swim towards the boat, which was drifting with the wind. He could still make it; he knew he could.

Then, with Jake clutched between his jaws like a dog's favorite bone, the crocodile exploded up out of the water, right in front of the boat Walt had been swimming for. In the few moments before Bill subsided into the water again, Walt saw that Jake wasn't dead yet; his eyes were alive and filled with the horrible knowledge that he was going to die now, and there was nothing he could do about it.

Blood colored up the water ahead of Walt. Walt turned his body around in the water and began swimming for all he was worth for the nearest pier.

Walt looked across the water, looking for a boat to rescue him; but they were all out on the far side of the lake. The solitude that had originally worked in favor of he and Jake's plan to catch the crocodile had now turned completely against them.

Walt swam on, closing the distance to the pier as fast as he could.

Oh, dear God, please let that damn croc take his sweet time with killing Jake, Walt prayed as he swam.

Walt wasn't being insensitive to his brother's plight. He knew that Bill's 'wasting time' with Jake was the only hope he had of making it to safety.

CHAPTER 30

Things look normal enough, Gary Bentley thought on arriving at the Teter Creek Lake parking lot. He parked his pickup truck, alighted, and then, shotgun gripped tight, ran through the rows of residential trailers towards the beach.

This was early Sunday morning, still earlier than 7 a.m. and so few people were out and about, which Gary was relieved about as he didn't want to cause a panic in case the killer crocodile hadn't actually come this way like Denise had said.

But Gary didn't really believe that. He'd left Denise back at Sleepaway Camp with the corpses. She'd wanted to leave with him, that was until he explained to her exactly where he was headed and what he was looking for there. At which point she'd shaken her head and climbed back up into her tree again.

Gary figured that by now the police would have coaxed Denise down from the tree again.

Gary slowed his run as he approached the pier. Several fishing boats were out on the water. Most of those were over on the far side of the lake, where the fishing was reputed to be better, but a solitary boat danced on the waves about a quarter mile from the pier he stood on.

Gary walked out to the pier's end to have a better look, and that was when he saw the man swimming through the water.

As the man swam closer, Gary recognized him—it was the older of the two brothers who'd crashed the van yesterday—the crocodile thieves.

But why the hell does he look so damn panicked? Shit, he's coming from the direction of that nearby boat! What have those two crooks been up now?

96

Gary aimed his shotgun at the water, but didn't see anything to shoot at. And yet the man swam on towards him, his eyes now revealed to be bugging with terror like he'd just seen the devil in the water.

"Help me!" the man gasped once he reached the pier. Gary immediately laid down his shotgun and reached over the edge of the pier to pull him out of the water. He suspected the man could have climbed out himself, but was exhausted from swimming over from the fishing boat.

Gary grabbed hold of the man's outstretched hands and pulled. The man's torso broke free of the water and he laid his arms on the pier to catch his breath. He stared at Gary with relieved eyes, as if whatever danger he'd trying to avoid had been safely averted.

And then, seemingly out of nowhere, Gary caught sight of a pair of glowing eyes under the water's surface. The huge orange eyes had appeared behind Walt Pollak with a suddenness that was almost surreal.

Damn! Frightened, Gary grabbed hold of Walt under the shoulders and pulled as hard as he could. Then he was aware of two things. First of all, Walt screamed like he was in deathly pain. Second, Gary felt a sense of reduced resistance as he hauled Walt out of the water.

Then he was lying on his back on the pier, and Walt was lying on top of him.

The problem was, Gary had only pulled half of Walt out of the water. Whatever had been chasing him had bitten away the lower part of his body. Almost like the dead kid who'd been hanging from the tree, Walt existed down to his hips, but both of his legs were missing. Blood squirted from his stumps all over the pier, staining Gary's uniform.

Walt wasn't exactly dead yet, but seconds were all he had left in this life. "That damn crocodile has gone crazy," he told Gary, with blood spilling from his lips. "It killed Jake too. It's behaving insane."

Then he was dead.

Gary shoved the dead man off of him and sat up. Then he slowly and deliberately got to his feet, afterwards bending over to retrieve his shotgun. He looked down at Walt's legless corpse and then looked in the water again. He squinted to the limits of his vision, but the nearer water was cloudy with blood and that further off was reflecting the morning sun.

Gary saw no sign of the killer crocodile, no scaly torpedo body, and no scary orange eyes. Where had the animal gone? Gary didn't know, but for some reason he suspected that it was nearby.

This is crazy, he thought. *This is just fucking crazy.*

It was truly weird. Here he was on this picturesque Sunday morning when most of the good American people were still asleep in bed, with a dead man beside him and a junkie crocodile in the water. He looked over at the fishing boats on the far side of the lake. Did he need to alert them to the danger they were in?

No, those boats over there aren't in any danger, he suddenly realized, a cold understanding coming to him. *Not at the moment anyway. Sure, our killer crocodile is hunting, but it's hunting for drugs, not people. If, like I'm certain is the case, the damn animal is strung out on Agent Orange the way I've seen happen before, then there has to be a store of the drug somewhere around here.*

Gary looked at Walt Pollak's legless corpse. *This dead guy and his brother must've gotten in the crackhead croc's way, that's all.*

Shaking his head, Gary turned away from the dead man. There was nothing he could do for him anymore. Law enforcement would be here to pick him up soon.

Instead, Gary Bentley gave the trailer park his full attention.

Now, where the hell in this trailer park is someone cooking orange-flavored cocaine? he wondered, knowing that that particular question was going to be a difficult one to answer.

CHAPTER 31

After killing Walt and Jake Pollak, Bill the crocodile swam back to the mouth of the river that had brought him to Teter Creek Lake.

This action wasn't a tactical retreat, as the crocodile didn't have enough brains to think in such complicated arcs, but was rather forced on the beast because the river banks were less steep and were easier to climb up than the lake shore near the piers.

Had Bill proceeded further across the lake he would have reached the beach and have been able to emerge from the Lake there, but the crocodile was now in a hurry. Now that he had dealt with the two humans he remembered, who had yesterday disrupted his lunch, those two competitors for his feeding rights, he was once more on the trail of the smell that had initially drawn him in this direction.

The Agent Orange was nearby. Bill could smell it, and apparently, the riverbank route of exiting Teter Creek Lake was a much faster way to reach the irresistible summoning smell.

CHAPTER 32

Max the chemist was on the receiving end of a particularly nice blowjob, when his trailer home began shaking.

What the hell? he thought pulling his cock out of Jessie's mouth. The next shaking of the trailer flung both of them across the bed.

Max stared at Jessie in confusion. "What the hell was that?"

She shrugged back at him, a mixture of confusion and lust in her orange-tinted eyes. She'd been hitting the crack pipe when he'd woken up and had volunteered him a blowjob after he'd commented on the half-empty package of Agent Orange on her nightstand.

"Oh, I just did a lot of rock last night," she'd replied. "Hey, how 'bout if I suck your dick, baby? You look like a blowjob would do you some good."

Now, staring at Jessie after their trailer home stopped shaking for the second time, Max scowled at the increased orange tint of her eyes. Sure, Jessie had great resistance to Agent Orange, but it was only a matter of time before the drug ate up her mind. And then she'd be very dangerous. Like other addicts, however, she was oblivious to the harm she was doing to herself.

Maybe it'll be better if I lock the drug away from her, so—

The trailer shook again. *What the hell? Are we having an earthquake? Or are the town authorities demolishing the trailer park?*

By now, Max had forgotten that he'd recently been enjoying fellatio. So too had Jessie apparently; she was already loading up her crackpipe with Agent Orange again.

Max located his shorts and pulled them on, and then leapt out of bed just as the trailer started moving again. This time the shaking was accompanied by splintering sounds and then Max heard the noise of breaking glass.

That meant the noise was coming from his laboratory. He felt a sudden fear. This was the primary disadvantage of occupying a trailer with direct access to the forest. Yes, the location of his home meant he had ample chance to escape in case of an attack; but as he was discovering now, it also rendered him more susceptible to attacks. Intruders could reach him through the woods, kill him, and slip away again, with no one the wiser.

After a disgusted stare at Jessie, who was trying to pull on a bathrobe while simultaneously smoking crack and trying not to set the bed on fire, Max got out a revolver from his nightstand and cautiously opened the door of his bedroom.

The laboratory was the third door, with the bathroom located between them. Holding the gun in front of him Max hurried to the laboratory door and peeked inside.

Fuck! The place was wrecked. Cabinets hung displaced off the walls, his previously carefully arranged rows of laboratory equipment was smashed on the floor, while the counters they had been arranged on were down on their sides.

But the strangest thing of all was what had wrecked—and was still wrecking—Max's laboratory.

The creator of the mess was a crocodile with glowing orange eyes.

'Crocodile' and not 'Alligator,' had immediately come to Max's mind because, before falling asleep last night, he'd seen an internet news report about a crocodile going missing from an Ohio zoo. And so, on seeing the giant reptilian intruder in his lab, his first impression was that this had to be the kidnapped crocodile.

That at least made some sense.

But why are its eyes glowing orange? Then Max sighed. *Oh, God, no. It can't be! That just can't have happened! Please, God, don't let that be what happened?*

Because if what Max thought had gone wrong really had, it would explain why he'd not heard anything from Toby and Denise since last night.

The crocodile had meanwhile stopped wrecking Max's lab. Having knocked the north lab window completely out of its space, its giant head was stuck through the wall of the trailer, which meant it had somehow leveraged its body up the side of the trailer. It swung its head left and right in the window space as if looking for something.

Oh, I get it. It can smell the Agent Orange in the lab.

Max laughed. *Well, well, well, who'd ever have imagined I'd create a new species of monster. Ladies and gents, I hereby present to you all—the crackodile! Yeah, crackodile's a great name for this thing.*

Max's lab animals were all quivering in their cages in the presence of this apex predator, their insignificant little rages bowing before this much greater anger. And they were all in more danger than they even realized. One of the brackets that supported the wooden shelf that carried their row of cages had almost entirely been ripped off of the wall by the crocodile's earlier raging.

Max stared at his giant visitor in an eerie stalemate. The croc seemed confused as to why now that it had arrived at this place, it hadn't automatically found the substance it knew was here. For his part, Max had no idea what to do. Sure, he was terrified of the monster crocodile, but he was even more terrified of what law enforcement would do to him when they discovered his laboratory.

I'm gonna have to burn this place down, he decided. *That's the only place I'll ever cover my tracks. And then, just in case, I'm gonna hire the smartest lawyer in the state.*

The stalemate between Max and the crocodile might have lasted for hours had Jessie not walked into the laboratory then.

"Fuck, what a damn mess!" she said, firing up the crack in her pipe. Then, on seeing the crocodile, she added, "The fuck is that thing doing in here? Ain't it supposed to be in a zoo somewhere? And why the hell does it have orange eyes too?"

The effect of Jessie's entrance with her crackpipe was immediate. Once it smelt the Agent Orange that Jessie was smoking, the giant crocodile stuck in the wall let out a massive roar, and then gave a mighty wrench of its neck that practically tore the trailer wall away. The beast reared back, this action letting Max and Jessie see how huge it really was, with part of the trailer's north wall now hanging on its neck like a collar; the shelf of little crackhead animals dangling at the end of this 'collar' like a tie.

Jaws spread wide, the crocodile lunged forward at Max and Jessie.

Max shot it in the mouth. The bullet stopped it, but Max's relief that he might have killed the crocodile was quenched, when next it opened its mouth extra-wide and vomited a pile of meat into the room.

The meat flew out of its mouth in a messy jet, splattering both Max and Jessie. Stepping out of the puddle of meat pooling around his feet, Max saw that most of the mess was composed of partially digested human remains. One of the skulls had a hole in it; most likely that was where the bullet had hit. So maybe the bullet had given the crocodile indigestion, or else it had dislodged the corpses.

This was also when the wooden shelf of little creatures that had been dangling on the crocodile's neck collapsed to the floor. Half of the cages broke open, freeing their tenants. The freed animals immediately ran away from the crocodile and with an addict's instincts, immediately headed instead for Jessie, who was still firing up her crackpipe.

On seeing this, Jessie staggered back towards the laboratory door. However, the sight of the human flesh on the floor had scared her so much that she was unable to take her eyes off of the monster that had vomited the mess up. This resulted in her missing her way to the door and instead backing herself into a corner, where the rodents quickly rushed at her, seeking the drug she was smoking.

She began screaming at them to leave her alone and tried to get away from them and reach the laboratory door, but then a rabbit bit through her left Achilles' tendon, and still screaming, she collapsed to the floor.

Once Jessie was about the same height as they were, the crazed rodents swarmed over her, biting, biting, biting, trying to suck the Agent Orange high out of her, because they were unable to understand the workings of a crackpipe.

Max heard Jessie screaming, but he had no time to turn and see what was wrong with her. Because, right then the crocodile lunged at him again.

Max got off one more shot, hitting the animal in the shoulder. But this time he was also unlucky, because as he fired, his feet slipped in the gore on the floor and he went down on his ass.

Max hit the floor hard. His gun hand smacked against one of his overturned lab stools and his gun flew away out of his hand. Now defenseless, Max scooted away as far as he could from the crocodile before getting up to his feet again. Behind him Jessie was still screaming, but he still hadn't time to spare for her.

Instead he focused his attention on the crocodile. Blood was dripping from its shoulder, and the wound seemed to have cautioned it against attacking him again, even though its huge orange eyes projected a look of rage at him that assured him that now it doubly wanted to both kill and eat him, and then digest him like it had the people on the floor of his lab.

But, Max thought. *It's flesh and blood just like me. If it bleeds, it can die. Two more shots in the head will finish it off. This time I'll aim for its eyes, so I'll be certain to hit its brain.*

On that thought he turned to look for his gun, and that was when he first saw Jessie. She was lying in the corner with her bathrobe open and was covered in those animals that had escaped the cages.

The little animals had ravaged her body. One orange-eyed rat had already burrowed its way inside her right breast, its orange eyes peeked out at Max from beside her right nipple. Two of the orange-eyed rats had eaten their way into her belly. They stared out from their holes now at both Max and the killer crocodile, their gleaming eyes lanterns of mixed dread and anger.

Another rat was digging its way into Jessie's left breast; most of it was already inside of her, all that Max could see of it was its kicking rear legs.

A rabbit was pushing its way into her vagina, its body almost half disappeared inside of her. Several of the other critters were feeding on Jessie's thighs, eating her up at a prodigious rate, one completely at variance with their diminutive sizes.

There was no hope for Jessie Barnes. She was leaking blood everywhere, and would be dead very soon. She still had hold of her crackpipe, but the left hand that held it lay limp on the floor, while a rabbit furiously licked the mouth of the pipe to salvage what it could of her last high.

Max would really miss Jessie, but at least killing the crocodile would be some measure of payback for her death.

He finally located his dropped revolver; it lay near Jessie's right leg. He moved to pick it up, but before he reached it, Jessie grabbed it first with her good hand.

"This is all your damn fault, you asshole," she told Max in an agonized voice, her face writhing up in pain as the rodents fed on her and burrowed holes through her. Max saw that Jessie's eyes were now completely orange, which meant Agent Orange had finally established full control over her emotions. "I'm dying, but so will you," she told him.

"No, don't!" Max protested, flinging up his hands.

But she did, pulling the trigger of the gun and somehow managing to perfectly place the bullet in the middle of his forehead. Max Carrillo's head exploded and his brains splattered the crocodile behind him. His body fell down on the mess of human remains in the middle of his laboratory.

Jessie Barnes died also then, with her eyes staring longingly at her crackpipe, wishing she had the strength to experience just one more transcendental Agent Orange high.

***

Once both annoying humans were dead, Bill the crocodile resumed ransacking the trailer hoping to locate the substance it sought.

CHAPTER 33

Gary Bentley was walking through the trailer park when he heard the gunshots. Two of them in quick succession.

He realized he'd been heading the wrong way; the shots were coming from behind him.

Gary immediately turned around and ran back in the direction he'd come, trusting his ears to lead him and adjusting the trajectory of his motion, when a third gunshot assaulted the previously calm morning.

But now, however he realized where the commotion was coming from. The last trailer before the forest began had a decidedly lopsided look to it, and as Gary watched, the trailer began shaking again; and along with the movement came violent hammering noises.

Gary slowed down. There was no sense in rushing into a confrontation with a drugged-up beast. His previous experience with an animal jacked-up on Agent Orange (and that had been just a little raccoon), had shown him how dangerous creatures became once they'd eaten the orange 'candy.'

So, holding the shotgun like it was a cross meant to ward off vampiric evil, Gary Bentley proceeded slowly from there on.

In the time it took him to arrive at the trailer, several trailer park residents who'd heard the gunshots had emerged from their trailers and were watching as he headed toward it.

"Hey, ranger, there's a dead legless guy on the pier!" someone yelled. "You know anything 'bout that!?"

"Call the cops again for me!" Gary yelled back. "Tell them to get their slacker asses down here fast!"

Gary wondered where his damn backup was.

Or is it that no one honestly believes a crocodile was responsible for the deaths at the Sleepaway Campground? It'll be just my sick luck if they think it's all the work of serial killers.

All this while the trailer had continued shaking. But the shaking stopped just as Gary reached it.

"Hello, anyone in there!" he shouted to the front door. "I'm forest ranger Gary Bentley investigating the gunshots I heard coming from here."

That brought no reply, so Gary decided to walk around the house to see if there were any obvious signs of trouble.

His fears were realized when he reached the rear of the trailer. Here, half of the trailer wall had been ripped away, permitting access into a room that, judging from the smashed scientific equipment on the floor, could only be a laboratory.

Well, now we know where Agent Orange is made.

Gary's thoughts clouded over when he saw the bodies in the lab. In the middle of the laboratory, a dead man lay on top of what could only be described as a 'human stew,' a mixture of partly dissolved human body parts, including two skinless heads.

Gary managed not to puke. He stepped into the lab, and as he did so, accidentally kicked a row of cages that had fallen on the floor at some point in the laboratory's demolition. He stepped back and stared in amazement at the caged rodents, all of them orange-eyed and glaring back at him angrily.

Avoiding the human pulp on the floor, Gary navigated his way through the lab. Then he saw the woman lying on the floor in the corner near the laboratory door. She was naked and had a body full of holes, out of which, several scared-seeming rodents peeked.

Gary almost threw up again. *What the hell? They ate their way inside of her just to hide? But hide from what?*

He realized it was a silly question. Those noises he'd heard coming from the trailer while approaching it, and the shaking he'd witnessed had been made when the monster crocodile was forcing its way fully into the building, in the process destroying the laboratory door.

With his shotgun ready to fire, Gary stepped as far as he dared past the wrecked door. He stopped well outside the living room, and from there tried to make sense of the sight of the sight of a giant crocodile ripping up an armchair.

From where he stood, Gary couldn't see clearly enough what was happening and he had no intention of endangering himself by entering the living room, so he backtracked out of the trailer, and then walked around the side that faced the forest to where the living room windows were.

After waving to the growing crowd of onlookers to stand back, he smashed one of the living room windows with the butt of his shotgun and after knocking out the glass shards from the window frame, leaned in for a better look.

He hadn't been mistaken. The giant crocodile, its eyes like motorcycle headlights, was ripping an armchair to shreds.

But why?

That question was immediately answered. After a violent wrench that split the armchair into two, a hollow compartment was revealed in the rear of the furniture, one packed full of packets containing a familiar-looking orange substance.

"Well, I'll be damned!" Gary said, to no one in particular.

Gary leaned his shotgun on the windowsill and aimed at the crocodile. He could see that the animal had begun eating the Agent Orange packages, and wanted to kill it before it somehow morphed into some kind of super-crocodile that could fly.

But the torn-up armchair was in his way and so, with an itchy trigger finger, he was forced to wait until the animal finished its meal and came up for air, which took a very long while.

Finally, however, the crocodile lifted its giant head and looked his way. Gary shuddered and tightened his finger on the trigger, waiting for the right moment to make the shot.

But then the crocodile began staggering about the living room, its body trembling like it was sick. It was moving in such an irregular manner that Gary knew he'd not be able to blow out its brains with a single shot like he intended. So, he had to wait for it to calm down again.

Which wasn't going to happen. Because, suddenly the trembling reptile froze still in the middle of the living room and both of its orange eyes exploded at once, first popping sideways out of its head and then blowing up like cherry bombs.

Gary was still staring in shock at this when the now eyeless crocodile slumped down to the floor and the top of its head cracked open, spilling its orange brains over the rug. A pungent stink filtered over to Gary at the window, like the creature had shit itself while dying.

"Wow," Gary said. "The fucking crackodile just died of a drug overdose."

He felt intense relief that the nightmare was over, but then realized that it wasn't, not quite, not yet.

We've still got those little monsters in the laboratory to deal with. Those little animals mustn't escape from here, or else . . .

With that horrible incomplete thought in his mind, Gary Bentley ran back around the trailer to stand guard by the removed laboratory wall.

He wasn't about tackling the rodents that had burrowed their way into the dead woman, but he could at least ensure none of them escaped from the trailer into the forest.

And so, he kept vigil there until backup finally arrived. And then he drove home to his wife Charlotte and told her everything that had happened.

And of course, Charlotte Bentley thought Gary was exaggerating everything until she watched it on the evening news.

The End.

ABOUT THE AUTHOR

Gary Lee Vincent was born in Clarksburg, West Virginia and is an accomplished author, musician, actor, producer, director and entrepreneur. In 2010, his horror novel *Darkened Hills* was selected as 2010 Book of the Year winner by *Foreword Reviews Magazine* and became the pilot novel for *DARKENED - THE WEST VIRGINIA VAMPIRE SERIES*, that encompasses the novels *Darkened Hills, Darkened Hollows, Darkened Waters, Darkened Souls, Darkened Minds* and *Darkened Destinies*.

He has also authored the bizarro thriller *Passageway*, a tribute to H.P. Lovecraft, *When the Bedposts Shake*, an erotic horror, *THE BLACK CIRCLE CHRONICLES*, a five-part mini-series that includes the books, *Prove Your Love, Strange New Powers, Night Wings, Sheep Amongst Wolves*, and *Lord of the Birds*.

Gary co-authored the novel *Belly Timber* with John Russo, Solon Tsangaras, Dustin Kay and Ken Wallace, and co-authored the novel *Attack of the Melonheads* with Bob Gray and Solon Tsangaras.

As an actor, Gary has appeared in over a hundred feature films, including *Faded Memories, Midnight*, and *My Uncle John is a Zombie*, and multiple television series, including *House of Cards, Mindhunter, The Walking Dead,* and *Stranger Things.* You can also find Gary in the motion picture adaptation of *Crackcoon,* playing Jonathan, the forest ranger.

As a director, Gary got his directorial debut with *A Promise to Astrid.* He has also directed the films *Desk Clerk, Dispatched, Midnight, Godsend, Strange Friends,* and *Shoulder Down: Road to Redemption.*

OTHER GREAT TITLES FROM

WWW.BURNINGBULBPUBLISHING.COM

"Lots of action!" — Kimberly Bennett
Author, Twisted Delights
GARY LEE VINCENT
PASSAGEWAY
"This is a book that will keep you intrigued to the very end!"
—Christine Soltis, Author Final Moon

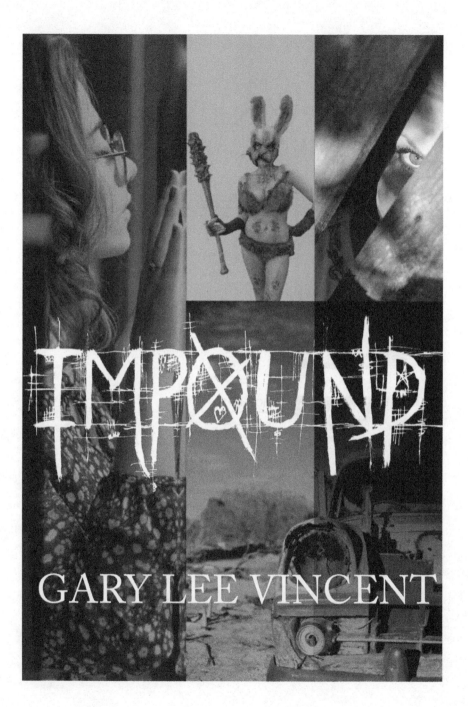

IMPOUND

GARY LEE VINCENT

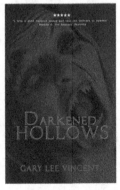

GARY LEE VINCENT'S
DARKENED
THE WEST VIRGINIA VAMPIRE SERIES

DARKENED WATERS

When the world goes to hell, the chosen must arise!

As Talman Cane orchestrates a flood of epic proportions in this third installment of the *Darkened* series the towns of Melas and Tarklin are caught completely off guard by the deluge. Hell-bent on finishing what they started, the evil brothers return to the lunatic asylum to take care of the witnesses and add to the ever-growing army of the undead.

Aided by Lucifer himself and the insane vampire demon Legion, the stage is set to channel all of the forces of hell to come forth. In an all-out race to survive, Jonathan, William, and Amanda soon discover they are up against impossible odds as Lucifer opens the Gateway to Hell, ushering in the zombie apocalypse and the End Times.

Find out who will survive this cosmic battle of the ages in *Darkened Waters!*

DARKENED SOULS

Melas and the Madison House are about to be rebuilt.
True evil is about to be reborne!

Young ex-priest and vampire-killer William is drawn back to the West Virginian town that almost killed him, where his vampire arch-enemy Victor Rothenstein still stalks the earth.

The town of Melas lies destroyed after the battle of the End of Days. But why is wealthy Jackie Nixon so eager to rebuild it using the bone dust of murdered souls?

Terrible evil has visited before, but the Gateway to Hell is about to be reopened in a horrific climax. And this time – it's personal.

WWW. *DARKENEDHILLS*.COM

Burning Bulb
PUBLISHING

GARY LEE VINCENT'S
DARKENED
THE WEST VIRGINIA VAMPIRE SERIES

DARKENED MINDS

Jackie Nixon intends to become Vampire Queen, but at what blood-drenched cost?

In this continuation to the explosive infernal saga begun in Darkened Souls, newly-turned vampire Jackie Nixon is taking no prisoners. Accompanied by her daughter, Kate, and by the captive vampire lord Victor Rothenstein, Jackie Nixon explores the Darkness. There, she intends to rouse the slumbering vampire race, bound under an ancient curse, and with their help, rule the human world.

But there's a deadly threat to Jackie's plans. Not just William who is trying to stop her, but her own royal ambitions. If Jackie performs the ritual to wake the sleeping vampires the wrong way, she could instead free the Red Beast of Hell, an unspeakable evil that even the undead fear.

DARKENED DESTINIES

With over 45 people missing after Jackie Nixon's party, the mysteries surrounding Melas and the Madison House keep getting darker.

Now, with legions of vampires at her command, can anything or anyone stop her from gaining complete control over all mankind?

The final battle has begun! As the Vampire Queen ascends her throne and sets to unleash the full forces of darkness, the fate of all things good hangs in the balance.

Burning Bulb
PUBLISHING

WWW.DARKENEDHILLS.COM

WHEN THE
BEDPOSTS
SHAKE

An Erotic Terror

GARY LEE VINCENT

STRANGE
FRIENDS

GARY LEE VINCENT

PROVE YOUR LOVE

GARY LEE VINCENT

STRANGE NEW
POWERS

THE BLACK CIRCLE CHRONICLES – BOOK 2

GARY LEE VINCENT

NIGHT
WINGS

THE BLACK CIRCLE CHRONICLES - BOOK 3

GARY LEE VINCENT

SHEEP AMONGST
WOLVES

THE BLACK CIRCLE CHRONICLES - BOOK 4

GARY LEE VINCENT

LORD OF THE
BIRDS
THE BLACK CIRCLE CHRONICLES - BOOK 5
GARY LEE VINCENT

From the Creator of DARKENED HILLS...

River
A VAMPIRE'S NIGHTMARE

GARY LEE VINCENT

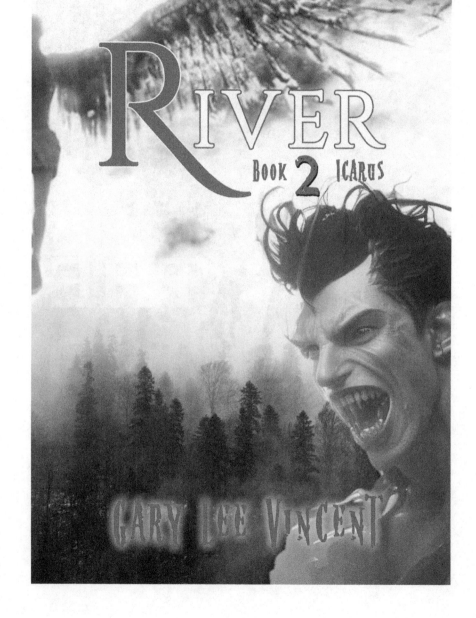

A Vampire's Nightmare Continues . . .

RIVER

BOOK 2 ICARUS

GARY LEE VINCENT

THE BLIND MELODY

GARY LEE VINCENT

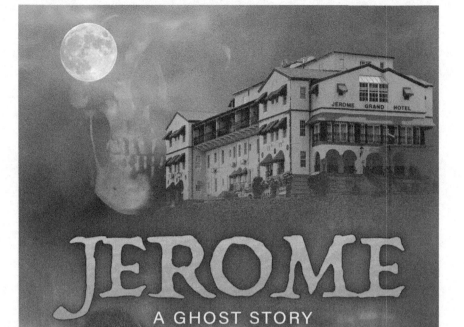

JEROME

A GHOST STORY

GARY LEE VINCENT

For more information, visit
www.CRACKCOON.com

Made in the USA
Las Vegas, NV
12 September 2023

77472861R00079